W9-BZU-390

You'll want to read these inspiring novels by
LURLENE McDANIEL

Angels in Pink
Kathleen's Story • Raina's Story • Holly's Story

One Last Wish Novels
Mourning Song • A Time to Die
Mother, Help Me Live • Someone Dies, Someone Lives
Sixteen and Dying • Let Him Live
The Legacy: Making Wishes Come True • Please Don't Die
She Died Too Young • All the Days of Her Life
A Season for Goodbye • Reach for Tomorrow

Other Fiction
Briana's Gift
Letting Go of Lisa
The Time Capsule
Garden of Angels
A Rose for Melinda
Telling Christina Goodbye
How Do I Love Thee: Three Stories
To Live Again
Angel of Mercy • Angel of Hope
Starry, Starry Night: Three Holiday Stories
The Girl Death Left Behind
Angels Watching Over Me
Lifted Up by Angels
Until Angels Close My Eyes
I'll Be Seeing You
Saving Jessica
Don't Die, My Love
Too Young to Die
Goodbye Doesn't Mean Forever
Somewhere Between Life and Death • Time to Let Go
Now I Lay Me Down to Sleep
When Happily Ever After Ends
Baby Alicia is Dying

From every ending comes a new beginning. . . .

Lurlene McDaniel

HIT AND RUN

DELACORTE PRESS

Published by Delacorte Press
an imprint of Random House Children's Books
a division of Random House, Inc.
New York

This is a work of fiction. Names, characters, places, and incidents
either are the product of the author's imagination or are used
fictitiously. Any resemblance to actual persons, living or dead, events,
or locales is entirely coincidental.

Text copyright © 2007 by Lurlene McDaniel
Jacket illustration copyright © Jakob Helbig/Getty Images
All rights reserved.

Delacorte Press and colophon are registered trademarks of
Random House, Inc.

www.randomhouse.com/teens
Educators and librarians, for a variety of teaching tools,
visit us at www.randomhouse.com/teachers

Library of Congress Cataloging-in-Publication Data

McDaniel, Lurlene.
Hit and run / by Lurlene McDaniel. — 1st ed.
p.   cm.
Summary: Events surrounding the hit and run accident of a
popular high school student are told from the viewpoints of those
involved, including the victim.
ISBN: 978-0-385-73161-4 (trade) — ISBN: 978-0-385-90198-7 (glb)
[1. Hit and run drivers—Fiction. 2. Interpersonal relations—Fiction.
3. High schools—Fiction. 4. Schools—Fiction.] I. Title.
PZ7.M4784172Hit 2007
[Fic]—dc22
2006012738

The text of this book is set in 11.5-point Goudy.
Book design by Vikki Sheatsley

Printed in the United States of America
10 9 8 7 6 5 4 3 2
First Edition

· 1 ·

ANALISE

I am floating in total darkness. Not floating like in water, but on a stream of air. Floating, trapped within a dark cloud . . . my eyes wide open. But there's no light, not even a glimmer, and I can't see. I hear nothing. I feel nothing. No pain. No brush of air against my skin. Not the limbs of my body. Not the beating of my heart. Not the sound of my blood rushing through my ears.

My heartbeat. My sight. My touch. Where are they? Where am I?

Who am I?

· 2 ·

Laurie

FRIDAY, OCTOBER 21, 6:15 PM

"How many times are you going to change clothes tonight?"

I stop riffling through the contents of my pathetic closet and look over at Judie, my best friend. She's sitting on my bed eating potato chips, spilling salty crumbs all over my comforter.

"As many times as it takes to get it right," I tell her.

"I've seen at least four outfits that look good on you. Why not just eeny-meeny-miney-mo them and get over it? He's going to be here in forty-five minutes." She glances at my bedside clock. "And I still haven't done your hair."

I want to be patient with her, but how can I? She knows that Quentin Palmer—Quin to the entire city of Asheville, North Carolina—has asked me, Laurie Stark, out to a bash at some mountain estate. I think of what Dorothy said when meeting the Wizard of Oz. *"I am Dorothy, the small and meek. . . ."* Freshman girls like me don't get rushed by senior jocks like Quin. And yet, I was. He came right over to the cafeteria table where I was sitting with Judie two days ago and said, "You're Laurie, aren't you? Want to come to a party Friday night?"

My mouth dropped open. I've worshipped him from afar since school started and now, just before school carnival, he was asking me on a date. Judie nudged me under the table. "This Friday?" Did my voice squeak?

"I'll pick you up at seven," Quin said.

"D-do you need directions?"

"I know where you live."

He gave me a smile that made my blood sizzle, but when he walked away, Judie said, "That's scary."

"What?" I could hardly speak and I was shaking. This happens when a god speaks to you.

"That he knows where you live," she said.

We picked up our trays and headed to the deposit window. I thought every eye in the cafeteria was looking at me because they'd seen Quin come up to my table and talk to me. I thought maybe Judie was jealous. "So then why did he ask me?"

"Because he's working his way through all the

new freshman girls at school. It's October and he's up to the S's."

I felt a flare of temper. "That's mean."

"Cool off. I'm kidding. He asked because you're pretty." Judie flashed me a smile.

We've been friends since fifth grade. She's big-boned and round with boobs that need a double-D-cup bra. I'm the tall lanky type with blond hair and size C-cup boobs—okay, a high B. Judie doesn't date anybody. I've dated a few guys, but dumped them when they asked for benefits.

People wonder why we're friends, because we're different. I don't know, but ever since passing from Asheville Middle School to Asheville High, student population just shy of six hundred, we've navigated the wannabe waters of popularity. *"With you steering the boat,"* Judie would say.

Now, with a date to a party with Quin, I see rocks ahead of our boat. But two days ago, I was walking on air. Quin asked me. Me!

When I tell Mom about my date with Quin, she practically does a cartwheel. She knows who Quin is. Everyone who reads the local paper and isn't mentally impaired knows. He's the star of our baseball team, the All-County and All-State team pitcher, member of *Parade* magazine's A-team, the number-one draft choice of coaches from Duke and North Carolina State and any number of colleges and universities across the country. Quin's hot in every way.

"Tell me how he asked you." Mom wants details, so I give them. Mostly to see her face light up. People say we look alike and I guess we do, but the similarity is only skin deep.

When she went to Asheville High, she was homecoming queen, Miss Student Body, prom queen . . . the list goes on. (My list is painfully short: cross-country team.) Everybody loved Lindsey Duvales, including my dad, Denny Stark. They got married and had me, but the marriage didn't work out, so Dad left Asheville for Columbus, Ohio. Mom sells real estate and makes enough money to keep us both in trendy clothes and decent shoes.

Sometimes I'm sorry she can't go to high school in my place. She likes it all so much more than I do, and now that I've got a date with Quin, I feel more like Lindsey Duvales than Laurie Stark, which is an interesting feeling.

So now, when I'm standing in front of my closet, all my self-assurance goes out the window. Judie scoots off the bed and picks up three outfits scattered on the floor. Two still have the tags on them from when Mom brought them home. She likes shopping for me.

"What's wrong with this?" Judie holds up a green sweater and a plaid miniskirt. "It'll show off your long legs. You should go for it."

"Too Catholic-school girl."

"Then go with jeans and this sweater."

"I hate that sweater."

"How about these jeans?" Judie holds out a pair Mom just bought, with ragged knees and a hole in one thigh. She looks at the price tag and grimaces. "Why would you spend this much money on something from the thrift store?"

"They're brand-new," I tell her. I snatch the jeans and slide them over my legs, zip them up. They fit like a second skin.

"This sweater," Judie says, giving me a pink one that has a low V-neck and barely skims my waistband.

I try it on, stare at myself in the mirror. "You think so?"

"I think so."

Quin agrees. I see it on his face when I come down the stairs, and it makes my insides glow. Mom has him cornered in the living room and is bubbling with enthusiastic questions. I'm embarrassed, but he doesn't seem to mind. All I can think about is getting out of there.

"You kids have fun," Mom calls from the front door as we start down the walk to his car.

I'm thankful she hasn't whipped out her camera.

"You two look alike," he says, opening the door for me.

"I've been told that before." I get in, stare out the window at my mother's figure backlit in the front doorway, where she's standing and waving. I want to sink into the upholstery.

Quin starts the engine. "Buckle up. I drive fast."

I do as I'm told, grateful for his blaring CD player. Now that the commotion is over, now that I'm riding into the dark hills beside Quin Palmer, it occurs to me that I don't know this guy and I have nothing to say to him.

I miss Lindsey Duvales. She'd know how to talk to him. Laurie Stark doesn't.

· 3 ·

JEREMY

I go in for a shot, elbow my way through bodies, jump and shoot and come down hard on Matt Trammel's head. He swears at me, but the ball goes through the hoop and my teammates whoop. It's just a pickup game in the gym after school, but it helps us blow off steam.

"Am I bleeding?" Matt asks.

Game's over anyway, so I humor him and catch him in a headlock, run my knuckles hard across his sweaty hair and say, "Suck it up. You're fine."

He yelps. "Let go, Jer!"

I oblige him. The rest of the guys have lost interest and are heading for the doors, where the janitor is standing ready to sweep the floor. The gym's open until four until basketball season starts, so I kill time on the court waiting for Analise, my girl. She works on the school paper and the yearbook three afternoons a week, and I give her a lift home. The rules are that the school has to be emptied of students by four-thirty. I'd vacate at noon if I could. But hanging around guarantees that I see Analise about every day, a hard thing to do now that we're both seniors with sucky schedules that keep us apart. And man, I *do* like seeing her.

I shower and change in the locker room, use half a stick of deodorant just in case the soap didn't work and head out to meet Analise at her locker. She and her friend Amy Cartwright come toward me down the long hallway. Analise Bower is tall and slender, not knock-you-over pretty, but interesting-looking. *"Dramatic,"* my mom says. Olive skin, green-brown eyes and hair that's a really dark brown, straight and hanging down to her waist. She never wears makeup, maybe some of that gloss goop on her mouth that girls like and us guys hate, but nothing else. I think she's beautiful.

"Hey," she says, leaning in to kiss me. "Can we give Amy a ride?"

I've been hoping Amy has another way home, because taking her cuts into my time with Analise. "Sure," I say. "No prob."

"You working today?"

"And tomorrow too," I say. Maybe Amy will get the message that she's a third wheel.

I add, "Mark's got a big cabinet job to get out before the end of the month. I said I could work tonight until nine. Maybe I can pop over later." I'm a carpenter's helper, and Mark's the owner of the business and my boss. He's trained me for three years to work with the saws, sanders and varnishes, and he pays me well. I like the job, plus it beats flipping burgers.

Analise stuffs books into her bag, slams the locker and takes my hand. The way she squeezes it tells me she understands my lack of appreciation toward Amy, and also tells me *"Thanks."* This is one of the things that attracts me to her—she sees into my mind.

"I'm babysitting," Analise says. "The Swartz twins."

"The pyromaniacs?"

"Oh, now, it was mostly smoke, and no harm was done."

Maybe, but since the "incident," Analise is the only sitter the couple can get to stay with the six-year-old brats. "When do you have to show up?"

"By six. I'm feeding them supper, and I won't let them near the stove."

"I'll do frequent checks on her," Amy promises.

I put my arm around Analise's shoulder and we head out to the parking lot. Once outside, she stops. "What a gorgeous day! Autumn's my favorite time of the year."

"I like winter best. More ops for snuggling." I nuzzle her neck to make my point.

Amy laughs, and Analise gives me a little shove. I grin. The air smells crisp and clean, kind of pure. Leaves are a hundred different colors on the trees, and the sky's as clear a blue as I've ever seen.

By the time we drop Amy off and go to Analise's house, it's five-thirty. I barely have time to grab a burger and get to Mark's shop. "Tomorrow night?" I ask before she slides out of the car, half afraid she has other plans.

"Chili night at the Bowers'. I'll have Mom set a place for you. And a DVD after supper."

"And after that?"

She gives me a sexy smile. "I guess we'll just have to see what develops."

My heart goes off like a rocket. With a come-on like that, I'll fly through the next twenty-four hours. Man, I love this girl!

· 4 ·

Laurie

The trouble with being the date of the most popular guy in school at a party loaded with juniors and seniors, cigarettes and booze is that I'm ignored by him. I spend a lot of time standing next to Quin and smiling like a stupid cartoon character while making a single beer last an hour. I've been smiling so long my face hurts. A few girls are giving me the evil eye and whispering. I'm starting to feel paranoid.

He's been guzzling beer since we got here, and his arm over my shoulder puts his dangling hand dangerously close to my right boob. I wonder if he's going to grab it. And if he does, will he laugh and tell me he's handled bigger baseballs?

"You want another beer?"

I swish the rest of the one I have. "No, no. Still have some left. Slow drinker . . . that's me. Slow as molasses."

His eyes look glazed, but I still can't get over the fact that he's with *me* and so good-looking that I could lick his face like a puppy.

"I'm going to the restroom," I tell him. He nods and I slip away.

The house is a mansion in the log cabin style up on Thompson Mountain, one of Asheville's mountainside golf communities, surrounded by woods and beautiful views. The owners and parents of the senior party giver are out of town for the weekend—which explains why the booze is so plentiful. I pass through the crowded first floor, desperate to find a bathroom. I ask a girl for directions and she looks me up and down. "You're with Quin, aren't you?"

"Yes."

She smirks. "He's a serial dater, you know."

"And I care about your analysis because . . . ?" I sound sassier than I feel. I'm aware of Quin's reputation for dating and dumping and don't need her to remind me.

"Because I was with him last party, and three of my friends have dated him too. He likes fresh meat."

I can see by her eyes that she's been drinking big-time, so I sidestep her. Last thing I need is a confrontation with one of Quin's old girlfriends.

"He'll dump you too," she says as I pass.

My face burns hot because her words sting. I don't want to be dumped. I enjoy being seen with Quin. I find the bathroom and fortunately it's empty. I go in, lock the door and lean against the basin. In the mirror, I see my bloodshot eyes and dump what's left of my beer down the sink. Quin Palmer's out of my league, and I know it. I also know Mom will be disappointed if he dumps me.

At some point, Quin says, "Let's go."

We walk through the frosty night air to his black SUV. My teeth chatter. I'm thinking he can't wait to get rid of me, but at the car he turns and pulls me against him. He kisses me hard and my knees go weak. A boy I once dated asked permission to kiss me, but Quin just takes what he wants. I'm not sure which I like better. In a way, it's nice to be asked, but Quin's way makes me feel excited.

He gives me his tongue and I like it. He runs his hands down my backside, lifts me for a closer fit. When he pulls away, he's breathing hard. I like knowing I caused it, but it's scary too.

He reaches over and jerks open the back door, saying, "It's warmer inside."

I know if I get in with him, something will

happen that I don't want. Not now, anyway. I have other plans for my virginity that don't include the backseat of a van in the woods. "I—I don't think we should—"

"Should what?"

"Should get inside." My face is flaming and I'm cold again.

He looks disgusted, slams the back door, opens the passenger door. "I don't ask more than once, baby. Get in. I'll take you home."

Feeling humiliated, I climb into the SUV.

He pulls out, maneuvers through a hodge-podge of parked autos and trees while I hold my breath and hope he doesn't hit anything. He punches on the CD and I stare out the window, knowing that my big date with Quentin Palmer is a bust, over before it ever began.

I must have nodded off because a *whump*, the screech of brakes, the crunch of metal hitting metal and a stomach-twisting lurch jerk me awake. I snap to attention. The SUV has stopped half off the road, the right front tire on the shoulder. I hear Quin swear. I ask, "What happened?"

"A deer. It just jumped out in front of me. I hit it." He gets out, walks to the front of the SUV, and in the blinding headlights I see him squinting at the passenger-side bumper. I open my door, but

Quin barks, "Stay inside. I'm just checking the damage, and there's a hell of a drop-off."

My heart's hammering. The cold air has revived me. I peer out and see that the guardrail is down, and I know that beside it is nothing but the steep face of the mountain stretching to a gorge below. I realize we could have gone through and over the side if the brakes hadn't held. I almost lose the beer I drank. I reach for my purse. "Should I call 911?"

"No. Just sit still."

I watch Quin drag some branches to the bent and broken guardrail.

When he's finished, he gets back in the SUV, slams his door, leans his head against the headrest. He's breathing hard.

"Why'd you cover the broken rail?" I ask.

"Because I don't want someone bumping against it. Lots of kids still at the party. None of them sober. They'll avoid the brush, and also the hole in the rail."

It makes sense to me that drivers will avoid the heaped-up brush.

He pounds the steering wheel. "Dad's going to freak. The fender's crushed."

"It was an accident," I say.

"He bought Mom this car for her birthday in June. I had to beg to borrow it tonight."

I can't imagine Quin begging for anything. "Deer run in front of cars all the time. It wasn't your fault."

He looks over at me, as if realizing I'm still in the car. "You all right?"

"Just shaky."

"Me too." He broods.

"Is the deer . . . I mean, could you see it? Was it, like, dead?"

"I couldn't see anything. It's black as pitch out there. I was just driving along and then it flashed in front of me. It came out of nowhere." He takes long, deep breaths.

"Well, if you need me to tell your father—"

He glances in the rearview mirror. "I'll handle it."

"My mom banged up her car once. Backed into a line of grocery carts at the store. You'd think she could have seen a whole line of shiny carts, but no, not my mom. Anyway, the insurance covered everything and the car went to some body shop and was as good as new." I know I'm spewing nonessential information, but I can't seem to stop myself.

"Hey, don't worry about it. You sure you're okay?"

"Perfectly fine," I say enthusiastically.

He turns on the engine, backs slowly onto the curved mountain highway and slowly winds the rest of the way down to the bottom. I can tell he's spooked. Maybe this is his first accident. Maybe his parents are really harsh. I want to comfort him but don't know how.

In my driveway, he comes around and opens the door for me. He hands me a mint. "To cover any beer breath."

Grateful, I pop it into my mouth and look to see the damaged front fender of the SUV. Mom hasn't turned on the porch light—to give Quin and me privacy, I assume. *Pathetic.* A dim streetlamp reveals that the front bumper and fender are scraped and badly bent. I get weak-kneed thinking about our close call.

Quin walks me to the door and I say, "I guess this is good night."

He hugs me, which surprises me. This is a real hug, not like the one he gave when he wanted me to crawl into the backseat with him. With my cheek pressed to his chest, I feel warm, snuggly, accepted. "Can you keep this our little secret?" he asks. "About hitting the deer and all. I'll have enough trouble with my parents. I don't need the hassle from my friends at school too."

"Sure. No problem."

He lets me go. "That's cool."

I slide inside my house, stand at the narrow window next to the front door and watch him return to the car, get in and drive off. I still feel shaky, but happy too. The date with Quin ended better than I'd expected, despite some poor deer losing its life. I actually feel hopeful that he'll speak to me in the halls at school come Monday.

· 5 ·

JEREMY

The sound of my cell playing the "Hallelujah Chorus" wakes me up. I'm in my room, my head on my trig book, and I'm lying in a puddle of drool. I sit upright and grab my phone. This is Analise's special ringtone. I picked it out because I want to shout *hallelujah* every time she calls me.

"Hey, babe," I say.

I hear a pause, then, "Jeremy? This is Sonya Bower. I'm calling about Analise. Is she with you?"

I sit up even straighter. "Um—no, ma'am." I was raised to say "sir" and "ma'am" and got smacked if I didn't.

"Please, Jeremy—" Her voice sounds tense and suspicious. "If she's there, let me know. I—I won't be angry."

My glance goes to my old Mickey Mouse clock, a relic from when I was six and learning to tell time. I keep it because it's kitschy. Mickey's hands point to five after one. I swallow. "Mrs. Bower, I swear she's not here."

I hear her repeat what I've said to someone else—Analise's father, I assume.

"Do you know where she might be?"

"She said she was babysitting. That's all she told me." My heart is thudding because disappearing without a word goes against the grain for Analise.

"Yes, but I talked to the Swartzes an hour ago and they said she'd left at eleven-thirty. She's still not home."

"Amy—"

"She's not at Amy's. She's not at Donna's, Tiffany's or Morgan's."

I'm standing, digging through the heap of clothes on my floor for my jacket. "Mrs. Bowers, can I come over?"

"It's pretty late."

"I don't care. Please. I—I want to be there. When she comes home," I add as cheerfully as I can muster.

"I—I . . . all right. Come on, maybe you can help think of someplace else she might have gone."

I hang up, scribble a note to my parents. I have

two older brothers, one in college, one in the army in Iraq, and Mom and Dad give me a lot of freedom, just so long as I'm honest with them and always let them know where I am. I stick the note on the fridge with a magnet, grab my coat and move as quietly as I can into the garage. My brain is spinning. *Analise, baby. . . . Where are you?*

· 6 ·

Laurie

"Well, aren't you going to tell me about last night?"

Mom's sipping coffee across from me at the kitchen table while I'm digging my way through a carton of yogurt. I'm still processing last night and I'm not ready to talk about my big date, but she's looking so expectant that I decide to throw her a bone. "I had a good time, and Quin said he did too."

She cocks her head like a bird, continues to stare me down.

I take in a large spoonful of yogurt.

"There must be more."

"I made it home by curfew."

She scrapes her chair across the tile floor and away from the table. "I was hoping you'd have more to say." She sounds annoyed. "If you don't want to tell me, say so." She stops on her way to deposit her coffee cup in the sink. "I just want you to enjoy high school as much as I did. I'm not prying."

She *is* prying; it's her way, but pointing it out will only cause hard feelings. I decide on the "give details" approach. "The party was up on Thompson Mountain. No parents. Lots of beer. And I drank some too."

I can see her thoughts written on her face and I wonder what side she's going to come down on—stern forbidding parent or understanding parent. I'm betting on understanding.

She says, "I prefer that you don't drink, Laurie, but I remember how it was when I went to school. We all did it. Just promise me you'll be careful."

Bingo! Can I call it, or what? "I kept the same bottle going all night." A little white lie, but she nods approvingly.

"That's good. No sense asking for trouble." She pauses, and I see her mental wheels turning. "Uh—Quin wasn't impaired, was he? I mean, I certainly don't want you in a car with an impaired driver."

I remember the deer incident and how he asked me to keep it between us. I decide Mom doesn't need to know. "No. He drank, but he was almost sober before we left." I tell her what she wants to hear.

She smiles. "That's good. You know, his father's the biggest land developer in the county, and I've sold many homes in subdivisions he's built. He's planning on breaking ground for his next one in the spring."

"Okay." Mom's real estate deals really aren't on my radar. They pay the bills and give her satisfaction, while Dad, in Ohio, is still a loser. At least, that's what she always says. He's never been into making loads of cash like she is.

She looks at the clock. "I have to clean up. I'm showing a house in an hour." She starts for the doorway. "What are you doing today?"

"Judie's coming over and we'll probably hit the downtown stores. Holidays are coming. Never too early to see what's out there." Judie's already sixteen, so she can drive, while I only have my learner's permit.

"True." Mom gives me a satisfied smile. "Let's go out for dinner tonight. Would you like that?"

"That's fine."

"How about Provino's?" She names my favorite restaurant.

"Any occasion?"

"Just because I love you."

"Good enough."

She pauses at the doorway. "Do you think you and Quin will go out again?"

I weigh the truth against what she wants to hear. I think, *Probably not,* but I say, "If he asks me, I'll say yes."

"You're a pretty girl, Laurie. And you're mature for fifteen. I'm thinking that he will."

She leaves and I stare out at autumn leaves being swirled and scattered across our back deck like dry scraps of old paper. The day's supposed to be in the mid-sixties. I decide what to wear and how I'll tell Judie about my big date with Quin Palmer.

JEREMY

SATURDAY, OCTOBER 22, 6:00 AM

Since one-thirty in the morning, we've been through three pots of coffee and a ton of "what if"s. I can't come up with any ideas as to where Analise might be. She hasn't called home or me, and numerous calls to her cell go straight to her voice mailbox. Analise's dad, Jack Bower, has put in two calls to the police, but they say until she's been gone twenty-four hours, they don't consider Analise officially missing. Teens run away. Teens get depressed and hide. He says Analise isn't depressed and she'd never run away.

"Are you sure there are no other friends to call?" Sonya asks me, after I make a list. "Maybe she has other friends you've forgotten about. She does so many extracurricular things at school."

I don't want to quash the hope I see on her face, but in truth, high school is like a huge social club. Most everyone operates in groups and spheres that never touch. There are the jocks, the artists, the nerds, the geeks, the brains, the do-gooders—the list is long and the school is big. I hardly know the kids sitting near me in my classes. "There's nobody else," I say.

"Then she's in trouble. Something's happened to her." Her knuckles are white, her hands wrapped around a coffee cup. "I should never have let her ride her bike."

It's the umpteenth time she's said this.

"Stop it, Sonya," Jack says. "It's a simple ride up to the Swartzes'. And they were supposed to be home by nine."

Analise's parents told me earlier that the Swartzes had called at nine to tell Analise they wouldn't be home until eleven. "I should have insisted that she let me pick her up. Eleven is too late to be riding a bike down the mountain. Why didn't I make her let me come get her?"

The three of us know Analise too well. She would have argued to get her way. She wouldn't have wanted to leave her precious bike overnight at the Swartzes' with the Destruct-o Twins around. I picture the shiny green bicycle. For her seventeenth birthday in September, Analise got a racing bike, a really expensive one with an aluminum frame and special gears for climbing and coasting in our mountains. She's a serious biker and finished fifty-ninth out of a hundred and sixty competitors in early October in a breast cancer event, which raised a ton of money. She snagged me for fifty bucks and her parents for a hundred.

"Whoa," I said the first time I saw her decked out in her racing gear, before that race. "I like the look."

"Spandex is not friendly to girls with big butts." She was looking in a mirror in her bedroom and assessing her rear end.

We were meeting Amy and some guy at the movies, and I'd stopped off to pick up Analise. "Depends on who you ask," I told her, patting her backside.

She ignored me, tied up her hair and shoved on a silver and blue racing helmet for the full effect. "I look like the freakazoid in *Alien*."

"My freakazoid," I said, and put my arms around her.

"Get used to the look," she told me. "This June, I'm doing the twenty-five-mile race in Charlotte for Special Olympics awareness. Be prepared to donate generously."

"Long race."

"I'm in training until then. When it's too cold to ride, I'll hit the gym."

I tipped her helmet back and kissed her. "I'm in love with Wonder Woman."

"Well, Wonder Woman has to peel off the spandex and get dressed for the movies." She glanced at her butt in the mirror one more time before shoving me out the door.

The jangle of car keys snaps me back to the present. I'm at the Bowers' kitchen table and pale light is breaking outside in the sky.

"It's light enough to start looking," Jack Bower says. "I'm not waiting until the police decide she's really missing."

Sonya grabs a jacket. "I'm coming with you."

"We need someone here—"

"I've forwarded the phone to my cell. If she calls . . ."

I say, "I'll use my car too."

Jack nods. "We need a search plan. Let's start at the Swartz house. You drive up the mountain. We'll drive down. See if there's any sign of her."

My nerves are stretched tight by caffeine and worry. We rush out into the cold morning air.

· 8 ·

Quin

My father unloads on me as he examines Mom's SUV. I'm leaning against the door frame of our three-car garage listening to him call me some seriously rude names. I parked the SUV tight against the wall, thinking I could camouflage the damage, but in the bright light of day, I see that the fender and front bumper are a real mess. I blast myself for not driving my Mustang last night, but Mom's car has more room. Hoping to score with Laurie, I thought we'd be more comfortable. I'm a big fan of advance planning.

"I'll bet there's two thousand dollars' worth of damage," Dad shouts. "*Two thousand, Quin!*"

Mom's in the house working on her second Bloody Mary and is steering clear of what's going on between me and Dad. I put off saying anything this morning until Dad was ready to leave the house. When he walked into the garage, I followed him out and dropped the bomb about the fender.

"How did this happen?" he asks again.

I've told him already, but he hasn't been listening. I say, "I hit a deer. It was loping along the side of the road. I swerved, but it darted sideways and I hit it." This is how I've reconstructed it for myself. In truth I never saw the deer, just a flash of white, which I figured must have been its tail.

He crouches by the fender, rubs a spot. "Is this blood?"

"Deer bleed."

"Where'd the animal go? You didn't leave it lying in the middle of the road, did you?"

"I didn't kill it. I think it bolted over the guardrail, but I couldn't see it when I looked over. Too dark." I recall dragging brush to cover the break in the guardrail where the animal crashed through.

He shakes his head, stands, snarls, "I don't want this reported to the insurance company. They'll raise our rates through the roof—which means I'll have to pay for replacement parts out of pocket. *You'll* pay for it."

I don't have a job because he says baseball is my job, but I have a savings account from summer work on his home-construction sites. "All right," I say.

He glares at me. "You're grounded except for school and the gym."

Baseball season is months away, but I work out in the off-season, lifting weights to bulk up. I need to have a good season to get the athletic scholarship I want: Southern Cal. As far away from this place as I can get.

"Were you drinking?" Dad asks.

"No." I see he doesn't believe me. "Yeah. I had a few beers."

"A few?"

"I was sober when I left the party." I fudge the truth. I *would* have been sober if Laurie had crawled into the backseat with me. But no, she put on her virginal *don't-touch-me* face and refused. I didn't want to argue about it. I was going to dump her at her house, return to the party and hit on Samantha Givins. I've done her before and she's not half bad.

Dad crouches and examines the SUV's tire. "At least this isn't ruined." He looks hard at me. "Was anyone in the car with you?"

Knowing there's a witness will really make him crazy. "Just me."

He nods and his expression relaxes a little.

"You're All-State, Quin. One of the most sought-after ball players in the country. You've got to hold it together this year, you hear me? You can't go getting drunk and smashing up cars and getting black marks on your record. Not if you want to play college or maybe even pro baseball. Your record's going to follow you all your life."

"It was a *deer*," I say in my defense. "I'm sorry. I won't do anything stupid again."

"You'd better not," Dad growls.

I watch him get into his BMW, raise the garage door and back quickly onto the driveway. A blast of cold air hits me in the face. I curse the deer and hope it's dead for causing me so much trouble.

· 9 ·

Laurie

SATURDAY, OCTOBER 22, EARLY MORNING

Dad calls. "How's my little girl?"

"I haven't been little in years," I say, not minding the way he thinks of me. He works on the Columbus newspaper as a field reporter. He's always loved journalism and writing but couldn't find work here in Asheville, so he moved there after the divorce four years ago.

"How are the grades?"

"All A's and a B in government. And I got an A-plus on my last English paper." I tell him this because he loves knowing we have that love of writing in common.

"Whoa! That's my girl! I guess the acorn doesn't fall far from the tree."

"I guess not."

"I'm already lining up things to do when you come this summer."

I visit him for a month in the summer, but

there's not much to do in or around his apartment. He takes off from work, but only for two weeks, and we go on driving vacations. I don't love Columbus, but I feel sorry for Dad because he's all alone. He hasn't remarried and has nothing to come home to. And I feel sorry for me, because I miss him a lot.

"Good, and not to scare you, but I've been reading a Chinese cookbook." One of the things I do is cook for us when I'm there.

"Not vegetables and rice," he says, sounding horrified.

"You need to eat something besides pizza and fast food."

"Says who?"

"Says every doctor in the country. I don't want your arteries all clogged. You have to walk me down the aisle someday."

"Ah, now comes the question: Anyone in particular yet?"

I'd love to tell him about Quin and our driving accident, but I don't. It'll only upset him. It might also make him call Mom to discuss it. Can't have that. "Not in my high school. I'm not Mom."

"Low blow," he says with a chuckle. "Yes, she was popular, all right."

"I'll never be that popular," I say, wishing I had a magic wand to turn me into a somebody.

"You are to me."

"Are you still coming over Christmas?" I change the subject.

"That's my plan. I'll take you shopping."

"I'd like that."

"I wish it could be sooner, Laurie."

He sounds sad, and it makes my heart hurt. "I wish you didn't live so far away."

"Less than a day's drive," he says cheerily.

The far side of the universe, I think. "When I get my license, I'll drive over to see *you*."

"Like your mother's going to let you take her car for a week."

"Maybe I'll get a car for my birthday."

Dad is silent and I realize I've said the wrong thing. "Honey, I can't afford a car for you."

"Did I ask?" My thoughtless remark has made him feel bad. He and Mom used to argue about money—the lack of it—all the time. "Don't worry about it. I'll get a horse instead. Then I won't have to cut the lawn."

He laughs. "Zoning restrictions."

I know our conversation is drawing to a close, so I say, "Dad, promise me you'll eat better."

"And you promise me that you'll have some fun in high school. Great grades are fine, but it's okay to have a good time."

"You aren't going to tell me that these are the best years of my life, are you?" I mimic Mom's voice.

"I think you get told that enough."

We say our good-byes, and he makes his usual promise to call me again "real soon." I hang up, still wishing with all my heart that we didn't live so far apart.

· 10 ·

JEREMY

We've searched mountain roads, bike trails and neighborhoods for hours but haven't found a trace of Analise. Jack's pressured the police again and they've put out an alert to their cops on the street. "We need to find her *now*," Jack says.

Sonya has taken calls all morning from people they contacted last night. Every time, she gives the same message: "No, we haven't found her. Yes, thank you. Keep praying." My parents have called me twice to check on our progress.

We're at a coffee shop, to grab food none of us want to eat but all of us know we should. My cell rings and her parents look expectant, but I know it's not Analise's ringtone. It's Mark's.

"Where are you, man?" he asks when I answer.

I remember that I was supposed to be at his shop by nine. He's got a huge cabinet job to get out this week and he's counting on me to help. I shake my head, signaling to the Bowers that the call isn't Analise. "Mark, I'm sorry. I should have called." I tell him what's going on.

"Aw, Jer, that's awful. Is there anything I can do?"

The irritation in his voice is replaced by genuine concern, reminding me that Mark is one of the good guys. He knows how much Analise means to me. "I wish there was," I say.

"Well, you keep looking. Nothing going on here that can't keep. And, Jer, let me know when you hear something."

I tell him I will and hang up.

Sonya begins to cry, and Jack pulls her to him. I look away because I can't stand to see their pain. My eyes feel gritty from lack of sleep, and my stomach feels as if a big cold rock has set up residence. I'm in a nightmare and I can't wake up.

"Come on," Jack says. "Let's go home."

Sonya protests, and I don't want to give up either.

"This isn't getting us anywhere. I want to talk to the police," he says.

We head out the door, me tagging behind like a dog. But I can't leave them. Not yet. They're all I have of her right now.

• • •

It's late afternoon when a patrol car pulls up at the house. We hurry out to meet the two cops coming up the walk. "Jack Bower?" one of them asks.

"Yes."

The air is sharp and cold, and someone's burning leaves even though it's illegal.

The cop says, "I think we've found your daughter."

· 11 ·

ANALISE

Light erases blackness. A high-pitched whining noise jars me and then, suddenly, I'm being pulled out of the darkness of my cocoon. I float up, up into a corner of a room, where I look down on frantic activity. I see doctors, nurses, medical equipment and then me. Me! Lying on a hospital bed. My identity returns in a rush, like water spilling over a dam. I am Analise Bower. I'm seventeen. I live at—

"She's flatlined!" a doctor shouts. He's tall with a red beard.

"Paddles!" another shouts.

I watch from my corner, curious, not one bit afraid. All below me is crystal clear, shot through with color and light. I feel no pain.

"Clear!" the doctor with the paddles says.

He places them on my bare skin, over and under my naked breast. My body jerks as electrical

42

current surges through the paddles. My body rises in a convulsion, returns to the table. I look like a fish out of water flopping on dry land, where I don't belong.

"No change," a nurse says, watching a monitor.

"Again," the red-bearded doctor says.

I'm losing interest in the scene. I become even lighter and without effort push through the solid ceiling of the room and into a long tunnel. I see a bright light and I feel euphoric, happier than I've ever felt before. I hear whispers too, and see Grandma Bower waving to me. I know she's dead, but I want to run to her, hug her. The tunnel begins to fill with the beautiful light, and I long to touch it. Yet I hold back. All at once, I feel unsettled, confused. A part of me wants to go forward, another wants to go backward. I stop moving. I'm suspended in the tunnel.

What's wrong with me? The light is beautiful and peaceful. I should embrace it.

A voice says, "Not yet."

Another whispers, "Go back."

I have no voice to answer.

I'm pulled backward through the tunnel, like a high-speed train in reverse. I zip through the ceiling of the room, swirl in circles above my body like water going down a drain. I struggle to remain out of my body, but it's useless. I'm going back inside, melting like oozing candle wax into my fleshly form. From far away, I hear the red-bearded doctor cry, "We've got a sinus rhythm, people! She's back!"

· 12 ·

JEREMY

We're in the ER waiting area and Analise is being treated by trauma specialists. The EMTs brought her in, that's all we know. Jack is talking with the cops who have appeared along with the EMTs, and Sonya is holding on to him. I'm hanging to one side, wishing I could crawl out of my skin and sneak into the back, into Triage, to be with Analise.

"Where did you find her?" Jack asks. When the cop tells him, Jack says, "But we went up and down that stretch of road fifty times. We never saw a thing."

One of the cops says, "Finding her was a fluke. She was on a little ledge covered by brush. Couldn't see her from the road. A highway crew was picking up trash, and one of the guys stepped over the guardrail for a smoke. He ducked down so he wouldn't get caught, and he saw something shiny

45

and realized it was the sun reflecting off metal. He saw a foot sticking out from under the metal and called his supervisor, who called the rescue unit. The shiny thing was your daughter's bike."

"How did she get down there?" Jack's question can't really be answered, but it's something we're all wondering about.

"It looks like her bike went over the side. Lucky the ledge was there. It broke her fall and kept her from going all the way down."

Sonya gives a little cry when she hears how close Analise came to plunging off the side of the mountain. I squeeze my fist so hard that I lose feeling in it. I picture Analise broken and bleeding on the rocks and underbrush.

The second cop says, "Good thing they found her. Supposed to go down into the twenties tonight."

"She was wearing heavy sweats and a jacket," Sonya says.

"Probably kept her from freezing to death," the cop says.

I think about her lying on the ledge all last night, alone and in pain. I swallow a lump in my throat.

"She was unconscious," the cop adds, "according to the rescue unit that brought her up. They wrapped her in thermal blankets to get her body temp up."

"Thank you," Jack says.

We're grateful that she's been found, but we don't know anything about her condition yet. Others are waiting to be seen—people wheezing and coughing, a crying baby, a small boy with his ankle wrapped in ice packs, several people propped in chairs. But we know it's Analise who's the most critical patient at the moment. We don't say it, but we know it.

I hear Sonya whisper, "Please, God . . . please let her live."

It seems like forever before a doctor comes out and asks for the Bowers. He's a tall man with a red beard and he's wearing green scrubs. He introduces himself as Dr. Kelly and pulls us aside, and I wedge my body in, like I belong. Like I'm family and not just a boyfriend. The Bowers don't seem to mind my being there, so I stay.

"We've got her stabilized," Dr. Kelly says. "She has internal injuries, a broken left arm and leg and a few broken ribs. She's suffering from hypothermia and frostbite on the fingers of her right hand."

"But she's alive!" Sonya's outburst startles the doctor.

He nods. "We've sent her for an MRI and a CT scan; then we'll put her in the ICU."

"Can we see her?" Sonya asks.

"Shortly."

I think the doctor is holding back.

"But she'll be okay," Jacks says hopefully.

"She has a head injury. A concussion, and there's swelling in her brain."

Sonya's knees buckle and Jack steadies her. "What's that mean?"

"We don't know yet." The doctor tugs at his beard.

I can't get my mind around it. What is he saying?

"Are you telling us that our daughter may have brain damage?"

Jack's question hits me like a stone.

"The cold probably slowed the swelling, and that's a good thing. We'll know more after testing."

"But we can see her?" Sonya says.

"Yes. However, she's in a coma."

"A coma?" Sonya says.

I remember reading stories about patients in comas. A bizarre story about a man who didn't wake up for more than twenty years. My stomach squeezes. My heart feels like a lead weight.

"When will she come out of this coma?" Jack asks.

But the doctor doesn't meet their eyes. He says, "Let me take you up to the ICU."

We follow him.

· 13 ·

Laurie

MONDAY, OCTOBER 24, 7:23 AM

"Listen to this, Laurie. It's terrible."

These are the first words Mom says to me on Monday morning when I come into the kitchen. I'm running late, and Mom's at the kitchen table reading the newspaper.

"What's terrible?" I sort through my cereal choices and settle on Cheerios. I would skip breakfast, but Mom never lets me.

"A girl fell off the side of the mountain on her bike and wasn't discovered until Saturday."

"A motorcycle?"

"No, a bicycle. It says she's a student at Asheville High, a senior. Analise Bower. Do you know her?"

I think about the name. "No . . . I don't know her." It's a big school, and I'm a bottom-feeder freshman.

50

"It says her rescuers found her unconscious on a ledge that broke her fall up on Thompson Mountain."

I think of the party up there, and that makes me think of Quin and how much I wish I could do the night all over again. I pour milk into the bowl, watch the Cheerios float. "Bet she was cold."

"It says she's in a coma."

I dig into my cereal, anxious to get out the door. After not hearing from Quin all weekend, I'm pretty sure our date was a total bust. I only see him twice during the school day—in the commons before first bell and when he's coming into the cafeteria at twelve-thirty. We have a ten-minute overlap. I'm anxious to know if he'll speak to me in front of his friends.

"She's in pretty sad shape." Mom continues her commentary.

"That's too bad." I take two bites and dump my bowl into the sink before heading off to brush my teeth.

"I can't imagine what her parents are going through."

I'm not listening now, only thinking about what I'll say to Quin if he does speak to me.

• • •

I miss seeing Quin in the commons. Analise's accident is all anyone is talking about at school. I still can't recall who she is. During morning announcements, the principal's voice comes over the loudspeaker. "I'm sure most of you know by now that senior Analise Bower has been in a terrible accident." The principal's voice trembles. "Her family has requested that friends of Analise please *not* come to the hospital, as she's in a special unit and no one but family is permitted. However, it is all right to mail cards and letters to Analise. They will be collected and shown to her as soon as she's out of crisis."

When announcements are over, the whole room is quiet, subdued. Even Tad Monroe is quiet, and that never happens. I must figure out who this girl is.

At lunch, Judie can talk of little else, and when I confess that I'm clueless, Judie says, "She's the girl with the dark hair past her waist. The editor of the yearbook. You know."

I remember her then. She was with the photographer last September when Coach lined up our cross-country team and took photos for the upcoming yearbook. I remember her hair. Who wouldn't? "Oh, yeah," I say to Judie. "Too bad about her." The whole time we're discussing Analise,

I'm doing an eye scan of the cafeteria for Quin while trying not to let Judie know how desperately I want to see him.

"I wonder how she wrecked," Judie says.

Just then, Quin walks in with a group of his friends. My heart does a stutter step. I *will* him to look at me, and miraculously, he does. I smile as brightly as I know how. His gaze skims over me without ever connecting; he turns to his boys and together they disappear into the food line. I sit with my stupid smile frozen on my face. I could have been a fly on the wall for all the attention he paid me.

"What's up with you?" Judie asks. "What's so funny about a bike crash?"

I feel hot tears well up in my eyes. "Excuse me," I say. I exit the cafeteria as fast as I can.

· 14 ·

JEREMY

On Monday morning, I run into Amy in the commons, and I can tell she's been crying. It's the first thing she says to me. "Oh, Jeremy, I can't stop crying. I just keep thinking about Analise."

Amy looks pitiful, and the waterworks make me feel helpless and useless. I think back to Friday, to when we all left school together, me and Analise holding hands and making plans, and Amy yakking about girl stuff. I don't know what to say, or how to console her.

She wipes her eyes. "I know you've seen her. How . . . how does she look?"

The Bowers have allowed me, and only me, to enter the ICU area where Analise is being monitored. I feel privileged. The unit is where patients with severe brain injuries—men and women with strokes, accident victims like Analise—are cared for. Machines are everywhere and nurses work the unit 24/7. Families can stay in the unit only for a set amount of time every hour before they have to rotate out. I'm grateful that Sonya and Jack have let me visit twice. At least I touched Analise, held her hand and kissed it.

"She looks like she's asleep," I tell Amy. I don't tell her that Analise looks busted up, her arm and leg in casts, with one whole side of her face swollen and bruised. I don't tell her that Analise's brain is so swollen that a neurosurgeon is consulting on her case. I don't mention the machines, wires, tubes, multiple IVs, the alcohol smell of medicines inserted into Analise's body. I don't tell Amy that I'm returning to the hospital as soon as I can dump school.

"Poor Analise. How long is her coma going to last?" Amy sniffles.

"No one knows."

"But she's getting better, isn't she?" Amy looks hopeful.

"She just needs time," I say. "That's what her mother told me. Coma patients need time to recover."

The bell rings and I'm glad, because Amy's questions are hard to answer. There's too much I don't know. Too much I don't want to think about.

My friends and teachers give me a wide berth.

The guys mumble, "Sorry, man." Girls and teachers ask questions. I hear later that Amy fell apart in class and had to go home. I cut out at lunch and head for the hospital. I have to see Analise. I have to touch her again, reassure myself that she's alive and coming back to us any minute.

· 15 ·

Quin

By Friday, I'm wondering how I can get out of being grounded. When I get home from school and park in the garage, I see that Mom's SUV is gone and Dad's car is parked in one of the bays. This sucks—I don't want Dad on my back all afternoon. As I pass his car, I feel the hood and to my surprise, it's cold. That means he hasn't driven it, and since he never comes home in the middle of the day—

"Mom!" I go into the house, fighting panic, remembering the time I came home from school and found her unconscious on the floor. She was so drunk, she'd fallen and hit her head, but aside from a big knot, she was okay.

"In here." Hearing her voice eases my panic attack. She's in the family room pouring herself a drink from a pitcher of martinis. I know it's

57

martinis because that's her favorite afternoon delight. "Hey, sweetie. Come give your mother a kiss."

I peck her cheek. She reeks of gin. "Where's Dad?"

"Charlotte. Business, you know."

She said the word "business" sarcastically, like it tasted nasty. "He took your car?"

"He's getting the fender and bumper fixed. You really did a number on my Caddy, Quin."

"Not me. The deer."

"Poor deer. It probably died."

"Why Charlotte?" I get her back on message.

"Bigger city. More body shops. More deals to cut." Mom sucks on an olive from her glass. "He won't be back until Tuesday, so it's just you and me, kid. How about we order pizza?"

I know she'll be asleep before eight if she keeps on with the martinis, and I sense an opportunity. "I'm supposed to go to Brian's. Homework."

"You two can come here. I'll get a couple of pizzas."

No way. "He's stuck watching his kid sisters."

She looks disappointed. "And of course you don't want to hang here with me. Serve out your grounding sentence."

I feel my face get warm. "Come on, Mom. Please."

She waves me off and buries her nose in her glass. I take out my cell and hit the stairs to my room two at a time, punching in Brian's number and thinking of who we should invite over to party with us. I remember seeing Tesa Jolley giving me the once-over a couple of times this week in lit class. It's been a while since we dated. Maybe it's time to hook up with her for old times' sake.

· 16 ·

ANALISE

They don't know I can hear them talking about me. They say my name, these strangers, using unfamiliar terms—edema, telemetry, NG tube, urinary catheter—but I can't reach out to them. I try, but I'm trapped in darkness again, aware on one level that there's something beyond me, pinned in place on another level I can't understand. I want to float out of my body. I want to see the light like I did before.

I have no sense of time passing, just an awareness now and then of rising to a surface I can't break through. I'm a swimmer, ever seeking the water's top side but never quite able to find it. I slip further below, working to free myself.

I hear my mother's voice. She's begging me to open my eyes.

"I'm here! Mom! Help me!"

"I love you, little girl," she says so many times into my ear.

"Come back to us, honey," Daddy says.

"Analise, Analise," Mom whispers.

How can I let them know I hear them? That I want to go to them?

"She moved her hand!" I hear Mom say.

"It's just a reflex," says a stranger's voice. "Common in coma patients."

"No, no, I saw her hand move when I said her name."

"Please, Mrs. Bower, your daughter's in a deep coma. She can't respond."

Liar!

"They tell me that coma patients can hear."

"That's often true. Those who recover report conversations they've overheard."

"So they can hear, but they can't move?"

Yes, Mom. Yes! Don't give up on me.

"Her hand movement was a reflex. I'm sorry, Mrs. Bower."

"She—she's our only child."

Don't cry, Momma. I'm here.

"So very, very sorry."

I struggle for the surface. The darkness oozes around me, like primal mud. I sink.

· 17 ·

JEREMY

I go to the hospital as soon as school's out on Friday. I ride the elevator up to the neurology floor, to the ICU. The Bowers are in the waiting area. Both of them. Usually at this time of the afternoon, only Sonya is here when I show up, and Jack is working. He comes after five. But now they both look at me, and I don't like their expressions. "What's wrong?" I ask. My insides go ice cold.

"They're prepping Analise for surgery," Jack says.

"S-surgery?" I sound like a snake. "But why?"

"The edema . . . the swelling of her brain. It's causing problems."

"What kind of problems?"

Jack answers, "If they don't relieve the intracranial pressure, her brain can herniate. It can push down on her brain stem and she could die."

"How . . . how—?" I can't get my question out, but Jack understands.

He says, "Her doctor will remove part of her skull to let her brain expand. When the swelling goes down, they'll put the bone back in place."

I feel sick to my stomach just imagining it. "I—I . . . isn't there any other way?"

"They've tried everything else." This comes from Sonya. Her mouth is set in a hard line and her skin looks as pale as paper. "There's something I have to do," she says. "I'll be back."

Jack and I watch her go down the hall and disappear into the unit where Analise lies. I want to follow her. I want to see Analise so bad I can taste it. I guess Jack can read me because he says, "She'll be okay. Her surgeon is one of the best and the surgery isn't difficult. We can see her once it's over."

"I—I guess I've seen too many horror flicks," I say lamely, trying hard not to picture part of Analise's skull being removed.

"She'll be okay," he repeats, and I think he's talking more to himself than to me.

There's something I want to say to him, but I'm not sure I should. I take deep breaths, screw up my courage. "Um, I—I drove up and down

Thompson Mountain a few times." He looks at me. "I went to the place where she was rescued. Where they brought her up. I keep trying to figure out how it happened. How she fell over the side. I mean, Analise is a good rider. She shouldn't have fallen. There's a break in the guardrail about twenty-five yards up from where she landed. So . . . so I keep trying to picture how it happened." I stop talking, wait for a reaction.

"So do the police," he says.

"They do?"

"Her bike's being examined at the crime lab. And the guardrail too. It was mangled and bent back, and there might be paint or marks on her bike that will give them some clues."

This was all electrifying news. "What do they think happened?"

"That a car crowded her. Swiped her."

I think about this. "Wouldn't someone know if they hit a person on a bike?"

"You'd think so."

As the implications sink in, I feel a hard knot of anger build inside me. "So if someone hit her and drove off . . . I mean without even check-ing . . ."

"A crime was committed," Jack finishes for me.

The click of Sonya's heels coming back down

the hall interrupts us. She's holding a sack and she's crying. Jack catches her in his arms. "I'm all right," she says. "I—it's just so hard, that's all. They're taking her to surgery now."

"Let's wait down there," Jack says.

I want to go too but don't want to be in their way. Sonya takes my hand. "You can come."

We go to the elevator, punch the button and wait.

"What's in the bag?" Jack asks.

She opens it, stares at the contents, reaches in and pulls out a wad of sleek dark brown hair. "Analise's hair," she says. "They had to cut it off for the surgery. I know what she wants done with it. Why she was growing it. I couldn't let it get thrown away."

I don't know Analise's reason. Jack and I wait for Sonya to regain her composure.

"Locks of Love," Sonya says. "It's a program for people to donate their hair to cancer patients for wigs."

My heart squeezes.

"Oh," Jack says.

"She was going to cut it off at graduation and donate it," Sonya says. "She had it all planned out."

My eyes get misty and I duck my head. This

sounds like something Analise would do: surprise us all at graduation with short hair to give her pride and joy to charity. I think of all the times I've run my fingers through her hair. Sometimes, when we've been totally alone, she's let me brush it with strong, even strokes that leave it as soft as silk and shining like mahogany. I like to wind it in ropelike tendrils around my fingers, gather it by the fistfuls and bury my nose in it. The smell of it, the feel of it, always turns me on. Once she asked, "If I didn't have long hair, would you still love me?"

"I'd love you even if you were bald," I told her.

"Bald?"

"As a cue ball."

Sonya drops the hair back into the sack, pauses, reaches in and pulls out a smaller clump. She offers it to me. "The program will never miss this much."

I take it, hold it like it's something holy. "Thank you," I say. My voice cracks, but I'm not embarrassed.

· 18 ·

Laurie

I pass him in the halls at school. Her boyfriend. Judie told me his name is Jeremy. He's cute. Brown hair that needs cutting. Brown eyes. Sharp angles in his face. Muscular body. He wears silver studs in his ear. I think he looks like a pirate, kind of dark and dangerous. He mostly looks sad, and I feel sorry for him. I begin to think that Analise is lucky to have a boy that crazy about her. I envy her that—having a boy in love with her.

I see Quin in the commons and in the cafeteria. Sometimes he acknowledges my presence on planet Earth. If he feels like it. It makes me mad because he has no reason to ignore me. I didn't do anything to have him blow me off.

"Except say no," Judie reminds me. "It's probably a word he hasn't heard since he was two."

Judie makes me laugh. "He could be nice to me. It wouldn't ruin his day to be nice to me." I tell her what I think about Analise's boyfriend. "She's in a coma and he's not staking out other girls. I admire that, don't you?"

"Face it, Laurie, Quin is only out for Quin. He's got an agenda and it doesn't include 'forever' with anyone in his high school."

"I know that. But just treating someone nice, being polite and acknowledging her existence . . . what's wrong with that?"

Judie shrugs and I watch her big shoulders roll. "Nothing. But I sure wouldn't look for it from Quin."

"What? No date?"

Mom asks the question as if I never sit home on a Saturday night.

"Judie's coming over and we're giving each other manicures and pedicures." I keep my voice light when I answer, although I want to yell, *"No date, Mom! Face it, your daughter's a social reject."*

"Do you speak to that nice Quin at school? Because often boys need to think a girl is interested before they make a move."

He already made a move. "He's interested in someone else, Mom."

She looks disappointed. "When I was your age—"

I don't want to hear another story about high school being the best years of my life. "You know what, Mom? High school's different now, not the same as when you went."

"Certainly, you have harder work and more choices, but the basic boy-girl stuff will never change. Trust me."

I grind my teeth. When the doorbell rings, I shoot off the sofa. Judie's waiting on the welcome mat, her face glowing. I can read her like a book. She has something she wants to share. In my room, I say, "Cough it up before you burst."

"I overheard Amy, that friend of Analise's, talking in the girls' bathroom yesterday afternoon."

By now, I know most of the cast of characters in Analise's life. Everybody does. "Go on."

"I was in a stall and they didn't know I was in there." Judie likes to drag out her stories. "Well, Amy was telling another girl that Analise had *brain* surgery last week so she wouldn't die! They had to take part of her skull off to do it."

I recoil. "Gross."

"Well, she's better now. Still in a coma, but alive."

I can see that there's more to Judie's story, so I wait patiently for her to get on with it. Finally I say, "And . . . ?"

"And the night her accident happened, the police think she was hit by a car and knocked over the side of Thompson Mountain."

"The police?"

"Yeah. Amy said the cops found auto paint on Analise's bike and on the broken guardrail."

"The guardrail was broken?"

"Pushed clean open. The hole was huge. Big enough for a bike to go through." She leans in closer. "And someone had dragged branches over to the break. Hiding it, the cops think."

Judie leans back. Her expression is smug. "It's looking like what happened to Analise Bower was no accident. I mean, not one she caused herself. It looks like she was a victim. You know . . . a hit-and-run."

· 19 ·

JEREMY

NOVEMBER 1

Mark's workshop is in an old barn off a back road in the hills surrounding Asheville. I can hear the whine of the big circular saw ripping wood before I walk in the door. Inside I see Mark feeding boards—poplar is my guess—into the whirling teeth. He's wearing eye protection and a French wool beret. His face and arms are caked with sawdust.

I love the smell of the place, the fresh-cut lumber, the mix of paints and varnishes, the dust itself. The wood was once a living thing and Mark treats it with respect while shaping it, cutting and sanding it, staining or painting it, turning it into cabinets or tables, desks or an occasional chair. "Chairs are hard," he has told me. "Most people won't pay what they're worth in time to make them." He wrestles works of art out of raw wood, and he's taught me all I know about his trade.

I feel ashamed that I haven't been to work for more than a month. I left him in the lurch. Not nice. Mark looks up, sees me, turns off the saw and lifts his goggles. He comes over, his face in a grin.

"Well, hey, stranger!" He shakes my hand.

I grin too. He could have been angry and thrown me out. "Sorry I haven't been around to help you."

"We're making it." He gestures to the back of the barn, where I see Rudy hand-rubbing cherry stain on a large bookcase. Mark uses Rudy only in an emergency, when he gets so backed up that he and I can't handle the workload. Rudy's a good carpenter, but he drinks and disappears for months on end. Mark needs someone he can depend on. That's supposed to be me.

"How's he doing?"

"So far, so good." Mark wipes the sawdust off his arms with a rag. "How's your girl doing?"

I tell him about Analise's surgery and how the brain swelling is down, that she's been placed in a room on the neuro floor but she still hasn't woken up. His face is full of sympathy.

"Is there anything I can do to help you?" he asks.

I drop my gaze, scuff the toe of my boot

through a pile of sawdust. "I want to come back to work. School just isn't enough to keep my mind busy. I—I need to be busier because I think about her all the time, and now that the cops think someone hit her and pushed her over the side—"

"What?" Mark exclaims. I fill him in on what I know about the accident—precious little—and he says, "How could somebody do that?"

"Thinking about it is making me crazy because there's nothing I can do. But if I ever get my hands on that driver . . ." I stop talking, let my anger cool.

Mark squeezes my shoulder. "I've got work for you, Jer. Let me know the hours you're available and I'll work up a schedule between you and Rudy."

"I don't want to take work from Rudy."

Mark grins. "He's been working steady for three weeks, so I'm figuring he's about ready to split. If the past is any indicator, that is. Don't worry about Rudy. Just show up. Spence Palmer ordered a custom desk from me. You know his kid at school?"

"I know of him. He's BMOC and doesn't mingle with us commoners. Not a big baseball star like him."

"Well, Spence wants the desk done by Christmas. It's a push, but with your help we can get it out."

Anything to help Mark. Anything to get my mind off Analise. "I'll be here tomorrow, soon as school's out."

· 20 ·

ANALISE

NOVEMBER 4–30

"I think, therefore I am!"

I remember from my philosophy class that a Frenchman, Descartes, wrote these words. I get his meaning now. I can think, but no one knows it. I am trapped inside a body that I can't make obey my instructions.

"Wake up!" No response.

"Move, hand, leg, eyelid!" Nothing happens.

I am. But also, I am not. I wonder what Descartes would say about my situation? Coma. Not dead. Alive in only the strictest sense. Time has become fluid, like a river. I am awake. I am not awake. I have no way of knowing how much time passes between these two states. I simply fade out. Or I rise like a bubble to the surface of a lake. Time melts. Voices whisper, then go away. I can't escape.

They feed me through a tube down my throat.

They bathe me, lifting my arms, my legs, washing away the smell of inertia. I never leave the bed. Mom washes my face, smudges my cheeks with a little blush. My hair's been cut, and she tucks the stubby new growth under a stocking cap to keep my head warm.

Daddy reads to me, like he did when I was little, until I was four and snatched the books away from him, saying, "I can read all by myself, Daddy." My old books . . . the ones I loved as a little girl. He reads them over and over and they comfort me.

A physical therapist, June, I think, massages my body, stretches my muscles, working around my casts. I hear her tell Mom, "We want to keep her muscles limber. We don't want her limbs to contract, curl up."

Mom says, "Show us how, and we'll help too."

And Jeremy comes and lifts my hand and presses his lips to my open palm, and inside my chest, my heart melts. Not the heart attached to my physical body, but the heart inside my soul. I love him so much. I try to remember the last time I told him that. I can't. What *is* the last thing I remember before I floated in darkness? Before I was pulled through the tunnel toward the shining light?

I struggle to see pictures from my past. If I can

recall something a philosopher said from a class lesson, why can't I see other memories?

"She's restless," I hear my mother say. "I think she knows you're here, Jeremy."

His hand caresses my cheek. "Wake up, Analise. Please wake up."

I want to go to the surface, but something is pulling me down, back into the dark. No matter how hard I fight, I cannot resist the force that draws me. One clear image glows. I am riding my bike and I see ground rushing past me. It's night and I'm cold. The ground glows with light. I turn and glance over my shoulder to see why the ground is so suddenly vividly lit. Blinding white lights rush toward me. Bright lights. So bright, I squint.

Darkness comes and I fall into it, headlong.

· 21 ·

Laurie
DECEMBER 5

I can't eat or sleep. All I do is think about what's been said in the halls, what Judie has told me. *Analise was a victim of a hit-and-run.* The police are sure because of paint scrapings taken from her smashed bike and the broken guardrail. I keep seeing this picture in my head of Quentin framed in the headlights of his SUV. I see him dragging brush toward the guardrail. I see his face, dark with concentration. I ask myself, "Did his car hit her?" It's hard to get my mind around it. If he did, why won't he confess? Why would he drive off and leave her?

"You are like so far into outer space!" Judie says.

We're shopping downtown over the Thanksgiving holiday, chased in and out of stores by a bitter north wind. My hands are freezing, and my heart isn't into it. "Sorry," I say.

"Are you honked about seeing your dad over Christmas?"

"Of course not. He's getting a hotel room and taking me shopping. I can't wait for him to come."

"Then what's got you so strung out?"

"I can't stop thinking about Analise."

Judie gives me a *Huh?* look.

I could bite off my tongue for saying what's been on my mind for weeks. Judie isn't stupid, and once she stares long enough at me, I begin to turn red. Now there's no hiding from her third degree.

"You're not telling me something."

I get tongue-tied.

"I think we'd better go over to Starbucks, sit down with some coffee and have a little chat."

I don't want to chat, but I feel confused and helpless. Maybe if I talk to someone—anyone—I can have some peace again. I let her lead me out of the store and down the street to the coffee shop.

She buys us coffee, finds us a small table in the back of the shop, and we sit. I sip my coffee and burn my tongue. Judie sits and stares. Finally she says, "Spill it."

Now that I'm actually about to reveal what's

on my mind, I get scared. "It's probably nothing. Just my imagination working overtime."

"You talk. I'll decide."

I sputter around until I can't dodge the topic any longer; then I tell her the whole story about the night of the party and my date with Quin. She listens while her blue eyes stare holes in me. I end with "I—I was half-asleep, so all I remember is feeling a jolt. He got out of the car. He looked at the fender. He covered the hole in the guardrail with brush. I—I took his word for it. That it was a deer. That he hit." My words dribble away.

Judie looks out the plate glass window, and I know she's thinking hard about what I've said. I'm feeling better for having gotten the words out, like a weight has been lifted off me. I take a deep breath and find that the constant knot in my chest has loosened.

I say, "I don't know what to do."

She turns to face me. "Nothing."

"Nothing? But—but I'm going crazy."

"Don't do anything *yet*," she amends. "Let me think about this for a while."

"M-maybe I should go to the police." I say the words but don't mean them. I'd faint; I'd throw up if I had to talk to the police. "I'm scared, Judie."

Judie reaches over, pats my hand. "Give me some time to figure this out."

Her willingness to help me instills a calm in me. I understand all over again what a good friendship is all about. It's sharing your problems and having a friend help you carry them. I could cry with relief and gratitude.

· 22 ·

ANALISE

I've been moved. I know because the atmosphere surrounding me seems different, and because I hear Mom and Dad talking. They say, "Long-term care center," and "More intensive therapeutic help." This means only one thing: I'm not getting better. Oh, my body is healing, because they've removed my casts. But my mind is still trapped, held captive by a demon called *Coma*. It rules me. I can't break free. And I've tried. Yes, I've tried.

Memories haunt me. I see the bright lights over my shoulder. It's like a film loop, going round and round, showing the same pictures every time, until I could scream. But I can't scream. I can't control anything.

Once, as I float to the surface of my reality, I hear Mom and a doctor talking. His deep voice rumbles. ". . . insert a G-tube. More comfortable for her . . . a simple surgery."

"We want what's best for her."

". . . best for long-term care."

I understand then the doctors are losing hope that I'll wake up. I panic.

"Doctor, look, she's moving. Thrashing!"

"Mrs. Bower, I know it seems that way, but it's reflexive. Try to understand. We test her regularly."

I want to scream at him. *"I'm here! You ass! I'm right here!"*

Mom says, "But her eyes keep opening."

"And she has higher brain function too," the doctor says. "Which means she isn't in a persistent vegetative state. We can see brain activity on her MRIs. But so far she is unreachable except through deep pain stimuli."

Mom begins to cry and I feel pain like no other. It sears through my brain, throws me back to the blinding lights, and all at once I feel the scrape of hard metal on my left side, the crunch of bone against metal as my right leg hits something hard. I see the world spin out of control and I am flying birdlike through dark space, spinning like an out-of-control top, tumbling headlong into total darkness. Above me, I hear tires screech and smell burnt rubber. I flail, spin, topple. And I silently scream.

JEREMY

DECEMBER 5–15

The desk is taking shape in my bare hands. Mark has created the four sides out of perfect boards of Honduran mahogany and now he's given me the top with a heavy bull-nosed edge to sand. I work for hours first with an eighty-grit sandpaper and a sander, then with smaller, finer grades, rubbing by hand until the top is as smooth as silk. Mark drags his hands across the wood and I stand aside, eager for his approval.

"Good job, Jer. Palmer's coming to take a look-see today."

I can tell Mark's not happy about this. It's like looking at a half-finished painting—unfair to the artist to have work judged before it's complete. "He'll like it," I say.

"Maybe. People with big bucks think the world owes them something."

I understand what he's saying. It's the same

with Spence Palmer's son—with a lot of the senior jocks. They act as if they're better than us. More talented. More entitled.

"How's your girl?"

"They put a feeding tube in her stomach. It's good because they can feed her better, but it's more long-term, you know?"

Mark squeezes my shoulder. "Hard, yes, I know."

"And they've put her in special boots. Contracture boots that keep her feet and ankles straight, and splints on her wrists and elbows too."

Mark shakes his head and I see pity in his eyes.

"But she's still pretty. To me." A lump wedges in my throat. Every time I see her, she looks different, less like herself. I want to cry.

"Are the police making any progress?"

I shake my head. "Jack says they're hitting stone walls. They've visited every body shop in Asheville and the surrounding area but haven't turned up one lead."

"What are they looking for?"

"Someone who's had body work on a late-model black Cadillac. They know that much about the vehicle."

"Can't they just check owner registrations?"

"They need probable cause." I use the legal

term that Jack used. "They can't just go knocking on doors and checking garages without a court order. It's possible that the car isn't even from this area. It could have been someone just driving through."

"On Thompson Mountain? In the middle of the night?" Mark blows air through his lips. "Not likely."

"According to dealer records, more than thirty-four black Caddies are registered to people in these mountains."

Mark glances out of the partially open barn door at his old beat-up Suburban parked in the icy gravel driveway. "Tourists. The place is full of them. Used to not be this way."

Our mountains have scads of summer people who show up every year, many who don't board up their second homes and leave until late fall. Anybody could have hit Analise.

"So, are the cops giving up?" Mark asks.

"I don't think so. But they have to widen their search of body shops, and that takes men and time. One detective told Jack they may have to look as far away as Charlotte."

Mark lets out a low whistle. "Lots of territory to cover."

"I wish I could help them out. I'd love to get my hands on the jerk who—"

"Anybody here?" Spencer Quentin Palmer III comes into the barn.

Mark shakes his hand and I step back. Palmer doesn't acknowledge me. I'm like the sawdust on the floor to him. I go into Mark's office, where the coffeepot is brewing, and pour a cup for myself. I look out through the small window at the two of them talking over the freshly sanded desktop.

Spence looks like his son. Or, I guess, Quin looks like a young version of his dad. The old man is fleshy, with sagging jowls. It's hard to believe I'm looking at one of the most influential men in our area. But I am. I think of my brother in Iraq getting shot at. He's a bigger man to me than Spence Palmer. And turning wood into beautiful pieces of furniture is a whole lot more worthwhile than being able to throw a stupid baseball.

· 24 ·

Laurie
December 7

"I have an idea to share with you."

Judie's voice on my cell fills me with gratitude.
I've been on pins and needles for days, ever since
I unburdened myself about the trip home from the
party on the lone date I had with Quin Palmer. I
think, *I shouldn't have said anything.* Then I ask
myself, *Why not?* Quin treats me like I'm a nothing. He's dumped Tesa. For the second time, according to the grapevine.

I say, "Can you come over?" It's Saturday and
Mom's off showing a house, so we'll be alone.

Judie says, "I'm on my way."

We sit on the floor of my room, huddled over
popcorn, candy bars and colas. I want Judie to eat
anything she likes because I want to make her
happy, and because I know her mother rations
these things at her house.

"So what should I do? Tell Mom?"

"I don't think so." Judie munches on a fistful of buttered popcorn.

"Then what? Who?"

"I think you should use this to your advantage."

My brain freezes, just as if I'd eaten a spoonful of ice cream. "How so?"

"How would you like to be Quin Palmer's exclusive girlfriend?"

"That's crazy talk."

"Is it? Let's recap. You and Quin are coming home from a party. He's been drinking. He hits something. Says it's a deer. You believe him. He swears you to secrecy. And you, thinking you're doing the right thing, keep his secret. He returns to school, pointedly ignores you, dates and beds anything with a skirt, goes his merry way.

"In the meantime, a poor girl from our school lies in a coma because her bike 'fell' off a mountain. The same mountain where Quin hit a deer. Coincidence? Maybe not."

Once Judie lays it all out in a straight line, I see how obvious it looks. Why has it taken me so long to see the big picture? I feel stupid. And frightened. "I—I can't just accuse Quin Palmer of hitting Analise. I have no proof. I wasn't fully awake when it happened."

"True. But he doesn't know that."

"I—I told him as much."

Judie shrugs. "So you lied. Tell him you saw everything."

"Why would he believe me? Especially after two months?"

"He'll believe you."

"How do you know?"

"He has to protect himself. He's a big name. He has a future. He has college coaches calling."

I weigh what she's said.

"You want to be popular with his senior crowd, don't you?"

I feel shame—not because of what might have happened to Analise, but because Judie's right: I want to be popular. "I—I guess so."

"You have leverage, girlfriend. You've got him by his gonads. Now squeeze."

Judie's eyes glitter and I see more malice in her than I would ever have imagined. My mind is spinning. What she's suggesting is . . . well, *blackmail*. I wait for my conscience to kick in, to rise up and be noble, to tell Judie, *"I can't do such a thing!"* My good girl lies dormant as I picture myself at Quin's side. *"There go Quin and his girl."* I can hear the whispers in the halls. I see myself sitting at the hallowed senior lunch table, going to the movies with Quin and his friends. Me. Laurie Stark. Freshman nobody. Bigger news than Lindsey Duvales ever was.

I drop my gaze demurely, not wanting Judie to see the beast within. "I—I don't know . . ."

Judie leans back on her elbows. "Sure you do," she says. "You know exactly what to do. I don't even have to spell it out."

It takes me two days to get up my courage. On Thursday, Judie and I arrive at the commons early and wait. When Quin arrives, he's surrounded by his friends and I feel my courage fade. Judie elbows me. I straighten. Clutching my books, I head straight into the enemy camp. If he sees me coming, he refuses to look at me, and that makes me mad. Mad enough to close the remaining distance between us in a few steps.

I say, "Hello, Quin." His friends turn to stare at me. Their expressions all but shout, *"Who's the skirt?"* I ignore them, lock my gaze onto Quin's.

"Um—yeah?" he says.

Cool. So cool. I want to wipe the smug look off his face. "Remember me?"

He looks me up and down, like he knows what I look like naked, but he doesn't, and I'm so glad that he doesn't. At least I did something right that night. "I'm Laurie." A couple of his buds snicker.

"Yeah, sure. I remember. What can I do you for?"

More laughs over the way he's scrambled the words into a lewd suggestion.

Anger builds again and my sagging courage is boosted. Judie's right. He *so* needs to be shot down. I say, "We need to talk. It's important."

I don't know what I expected, but it wasn't watching Quin turn as white as chalk and look sick to his stomach over my pronouncement.

· 25 ·

Quin

I hardly ever get taken out of my game. But Laurie's words did it. *"We have to talk."* My mind flashes back to the long-ago day I heard them fall from Corrine Ochoa's lips. It was at the end of eighth grade and I had just made the first-string All-City All-Stars senior baseball team. A big deal because no fourteen-year-old had ever made it before. Dad made sure every paper in the area carried the story. My parents let me throw a pool party. Everyone came—my friends, their friends. And Cory came too. Beautiful, dark-haired Cory, the girl I loved. My girl. And in the middle of the party, she walked up to me and said, "We have to talk."

"Can't it wait? Dad's passing out burgers."

"It can't wait. And I'm not hungry."

And something in her voice, in her face, told

me that what she had to say was serious. "Let's go in the house. Less noise."

I was wet from swimming, and when we stepped inside the air-conditioned family room, goose bumps covered me. I pulled Cory to me, kissed her like I had a hundred times before. Her body went rigid. "Hey," I said, "where's my girl?"

"She's here." Yet Cory pushed away and I saw tears in her eyes.

"What's wrong?" She was scaring me, because Cory was always sunshine and smiles and softness in my arms. She was the first girl I had sex with, the only girl I've ever loved. Our bodies fit together like puzzle pieces.

"Quin, I'm pregnant."

Her words fell like dark raindrops on my heart. "Are . . . are you sure?"

"I took the home test three times. I'm sure." She started to cry. "My parents will kill me."

I took her in my arms. "Hey, it's not the end of the world."

She looked up at me, her eyes brimming. "You're not mad?"

"I—I don't think so." I held her tight. I wasn't mad. I wanted her so much.

"What are we going to do?"

"I don't know. We'll figure it out." My insides

turned to jelly. I would have married her the next day. I knew I had to tell my father. And that scared me more.

Laurie won't tell me what's on her mind. She says she needs more time than five minutes before first bell. I indulge her, throw her a bone. "I'll drive you home." She agrees and walks away. I watch her, remind myself that she's still good-looking and that I'd like to sample the parts of her she kept hidden on our first date. I'm between girlfriends, and I like a challenge.

When she gets into my Mustang after school, she's quiet, so I try to get her talking. When I pull into her driveway, she sits sideways, leaning against the passenger door. Just out of reach.

"So what's so important?" I ask.

She's nervous, but she tells me, and the longer she talks, the sicker I get. "There was no deer, Quin. You hit that girl," she says. "I know you did. And you know you did."

"That's a lie!" I want to slap her, but I'm frozen. The memory sweeps over me. The road winding and dark, lit only by the bright white of the headlights. I'm seeing double, but still, I'm certain I can drive just fine. Everything's blurry, and when I glance over at Laurie, I can swear she's asleep. Then I feel the awful bump, hear the shearing of metal. I stomp on the brake, almost veering off the side of the mountain. But I hold the car on the dirty, weed-choked shoulder of the road, back up, come to a stop and jump out. The fender's a mess, smeared with wetness and scraped clean of paint. A few yards ahead, I see a gaping hole in the guardrail. Laurie is getting out of the car, but I make her stay inside. Stone-cold sober now, I go to the break in the guardrail and peer over the side into absolute darkness. I see nothing.

Looking at Laurie now, I break out in a cold sweat. "It was a deer," I tell her. "I swear to God, it was a deer."

"It was Analise Bower," Laurie says to me. "You just *assumed* it was a deer."

Her eyes are like hard blue marbles, and suddenly, I'm not so sure of anything. If she's right . . . if it was Analise . . . I want to puke. "You can't *prove* anything."

"I don't need to. All I have to do is tell the story and you're a suspect."

Of course she's right. *Bye-bye college scholarships.* No coach wants a pariah, and that's what I'll be if word gets out that I was the driver in a hit-and-run. I stare at her long and hard. She's not so attractive to me anymore. "What do you want?" I recognize that this is a negotiation. I know about negotiations because my father does deals all the time.

"Easy one for you. I want to be your new girl-friend."

I'm speechless. How simple is that? "And?"

"And we're an item one hundred percent of the time."

I think about this and have the sense to know it isn't that simple, but at the moment my brain's in a tailspin. I consider my options, and only one pops up—the one I don't want to have to take. I can tell my father. I discard it like a bad taste in my mouth. Having Laurie hang around might work for me.

Before I can speak, she adds, "*Exclusive* item."

"For how long?"

"Until you graduate."

Six months. "Okay," I say, thinking I'm getting off easy.

She exits the car. "Then pick me up tomorrow morning for school."

"Hey, wait. I've got—"

She leans in the window. "You've got me first."

· 26 ·

Laurie

DECEMBER 12

"Did Quin Palmer bring you home?"

Mom's waiting for me, ready to pounce, when I walk into the house.

"Yes," I say.

She smiles so big, all her teeth show. "Tell me more."

"We've worked out some problems we've had, and he wants me to be his exclusive girlfriend."

"I just *knew* you could work it out with him!"

My insides are churning like boiling soup. She follows me into the kitchen, where I drop my books and take a cola out of the fridge. "You were right," I say. "We worked it out."

For a second, I think she's going to jump up and down and clap.

"I've got homework," I tell her.

She looks disappointed, like she was expecting me to tell her all the juicy details of my wonderful reunion with Quin. I want to run upstairs and call Judie. She foresaw this ending days ago: Quin caved. I pulled it off! I kept my cool and made my deal, just like playing a hand of poker.

I take my cola and my books and go upstairs. In the quiet of my room, I begin to shake. I conjure up the expression on his face when I announced my terms. First relief, then the look of a cornered animal. I see myself as rich and famous one day and able to get away with anything. I picture a reporter shoving a mike under my nose. "So, Ms. Stark, tell us about your first boyfriend. Wasn't he baseball great Quin Palmer?"

"He was."

"Isn't it true that you bought him with a threat to ruin his life?"

"It worked like a charm. He was mine for six whole months."

"How clever of you. How unprincipled."

Who am I? What have I become?

I search for my cell because I know Judie is waiting for my call. My hands are shaking so badly, I can't punch in a text message. My stomach heaves. I run to the bathroom, I lean over the bowl and I throw up.

· 27 ·

JEREMY

DECEMBER 15

When school's out for the holidays, I visit Analise one Monday morning at the facility. This is
Analise's home now. I know all the employees,
the caregivers who make sure the brain-injured
residents are fed, bathed, groomed and stimulated.
The desk nurse waves to me and I nod to her.

I go directly to Analise's room and see her sitting up in a chair. My heart leaps, but then I notice that she's propped in the chair, secured with a
belt and surrounded by pillows. Sonya is reading
to Analise from a stack of cards and letters in her
lap. When Sonya sees me, she smiles and says to
Analise, "Oh, look, honey! Look who's come to
visit. It's Jeremy." I hate the way Sonya talks
to Analise, like a mother with a not-too-bright
child. "*She's not an imbecile,*" I want to say. "*Her
mind's just in lockdown.*" I crouch in front of the

chair, take her hand and kiss it. "Hi, baby," I say in my softest, most adult voice.

Her eyes are open and her gaze is darting, but we know she's seeing nothing.

I ask Sonya, "Why is she in the chair?"

Her face gets red. "The nurses are humoring me. I—I just wanted to see if . . . if it might make a difference."

I can tell by her expression that there's been no change. I ask, "What are you reading?"

"Christmas cards, get-well cards." Sonya points to a cardboard box in a corner. "She gets so many. I had no idea she had so many friends. I—I thought if she can hear me, she'll be happy knowing so many people are thinking about her, praying for her." She looks at me. "I'm thinking of letting a few of her closest friends come in and visit." Up until now, Sonya and Jack have shielded Analise, watched over her as fiercely as guard dogs. "Especially Amy. She calls every day. What do you think, Jeremy? Do you think it's a good idea?"

I don't want anyone staring at Analise, carrying stories of her condition back to school. Stories of how her face has changed; how her jaw sticks out because of the clenching of her teeth, which the doctors can't control; how her gaze darts without purpose. We've had time to adjust to the changes in her body, but others haven't. Seeing her as she is now will be a jolt. "Maybe Amy," I say. "She can be trusted."

Sonya nods. "Amy's asked me for a few baby pictures of Analise for the yearbook. She and the staff are setting aside several pages to pay tribute to our girl." She shifts the mail to a nearby table. "Any special plans for Christmas?" She changes the subject.

"Both my brothers will be home for the holidays. Mom's cooking up a storm."

"That'll be so nice."

Tears brim in Sonya's eyes, and I quickly look away. She says, "Who'd ever have thought we'd be spending Christmas in a place like this? I—I'm grateful for it," she adds quickly. "The staff is wonderful. It's just that I thought we'd all be at the house, the three of us. Now it doesn't look as if she'll be home . . . ever."

"Don't say that."

She looks at Analise, strokes her arm. "I get so discouraged sometimes. And you know what really makes me angry, Jeremy?" She doesn't wait for me to answer. "It's knowing that somewhere out there, someone is walking around, planning Christmas, maybe with their family, just going along fancy-free, *knowing* they have struck our little girl on her bike and driven off without so much as a backward glance."

I feel my own anger boil up as I too see the picture Sonya has painted. Analise's eyes continue to dart, but they look blank and purposeless. I remember how her eyes once twinkled, brimmed with intelligence and fire. And love. I shudder.

Sonya says, "Someone has ruined her life. Ruined our lives. Yours too. And even Amy's been permanently affected. It isn't right, Jeremy. It isn't right."

She's crying now and I'm helpless to do anything to make her feel better. There's nothing I can say. I mutter a curse on the person or persons who did this to Analise . . . did this to all of us. I hope they burn in hell.

· 28 ·

ANALISE

I feel Jeremy's kiss on my hand. I want to tell him I love him. I want to let him know how happy I am whenever he comes into the room. If my thoughts could reach out and touch him, they would cover him in kisses. If I could control my body . . . if I could move . . . Stop it! I can't move. The only thing that makes this bearable is that time is fluid. I sleep. I wake. Great chunks of time pass in between. I never know when my consciousness will rise to the surface. I only know that it does. And when it does, I hear them talking. Mom's pain hits my soul and makes me angry. I struggle to speak.

I hear Mom say, "She's agitated, Jeremy. Help me get her into bed."

"This is just a *reflex*?"

"That's what the doctors say, but they're wrong, Jeremy. I know they are."

104

They lift me, my mother and my love. They lay me down on clean linen, cover me, kiss my cheeks, stroke my arms, trying to calm me. They whisper my name. I want to cry. I want to tell them how much I love them. Someone did this to me. Someone who's still out there. And now I want something else.

I want revenge.

· 29 ·

JEREMY

I help Mark carry the massive desk into Spencer Palmer's den. We've driven it over in Mark's pickup, brushed the falling snow off the tarp covering it in the circular driveway. The front doors of the Palmer mansion—because it looks like a mansion to me—are double wide, but even so, we had to remove the desk's top to get the piece safely inside. We could have used Rudy's help, but he hasn't come to work for two weeks, so Mark figures we won't see him again for quite a while.

The den is off the foyer, close to the front doors. "Here," Mrs. Palmer says, indicating a place near a bay window. "He told me to have you place it here."

We do as we're told. "Now for the top," Mark says. "I'll bolt it in place."

"Whatever," she says.

I glance at her from the corner of my eye. She's

a pretty woman, blond like Quin, but her eyes look dull. Not vacant like Analise's eyes, but not full of energy either.

We place the top on the desk and Mark crawls underneath with his cordless drill and bolts it into place. In the room's light, the mahogany surface gleams. I've brushed on seven coats of satin varnish and sanded with extra-fine paper between applications. I can almost see my reflection.

Mark's finishing up when the front door opens and Quin and some girl walk in. Quin sticks his head into the den. "Hey, Mom. What's up?"

"Your dad's new desk," she says.

Quin takes the girl's arm and they come into the den. "Let me see."

I stand aside. I've seen the girl before at school, but I don't know her name. She glances at me, looks nervous, glances away. I wonder what her problem is.

"Sweet," Quin says over the desk. He looks at me. "You do this?"

"I just helped."

The girl is jumpy and acts like she wants to bolt. Maybe it's hard for her to be around common people.

Mark takes a final swipe with a clean rag over the top of the desk. "I guess that's it."

"Spence will be in touch," Quin's mother says.

We go to the door and I take one final look at the room, the desk and the people. Quin and his mother are talking, but the girl is looking straight at me. Her eyes are wide. She looks for all the world as if she's seeing a ghost.

Quin
December 25

"*That's* my Christmas present? A new car?"

Mom's hot, madder than I've seen her in a long time, and she's yelling at Dad. A great way to start off Christmas morning.

"Is this how you say thank you, Carla?"

"You bought me a new car for my birthday in June. I've hardly driven it. The tires aren't even dirty. I don't want a new car!" She tosses the keys to her brand-new Lexus onto the floor.

"You'll like this one too. Stop complaining."

Dad's face looks red, and veins are bulging in his neck. I sit on the sofa, a box with a new sweater open in my lap. *Forget I'm here*, I think.

"What was wrong with my SUV?" Mom yells.

"Did you forget? It was in an accident."

Uh-oh. My fault. I glare at my father.

"It was a fender," Mom says slowly, deliberately. "You had it replaced. Good as new."

"The car took a wallop and it could have developed problems in the long term."

"Well, why not wait until then?"

I tune them out and feel a prickle of cold sweat along my upper lip. Dad couldn't know about my accident. Not the version Laurie claims is true. Just because Analise and I were in the same vicinity at the same time doesn't mean I hit her. I swallow hard. If I wasn't afraid it might be true, then I wouldn't have let Laurie take over my life, now, would I? I already hate being involved with her. We've been together every night since school let out, and neither of us has had a good time. She's uptight and bitchy. If I try to touch her, she pushes me away.

I say, "Look, you owe me certain rights if you're going to be my girl."

She says, "I owe you nothing. Keep your hands to yourself."

I hate thinking about school starting up again in January and her playing my girlfriend. But I don't know how to get out of it.

The slamming of a door brings me back into the present, to Christmas morning at the Palmer house. Dad's gone; Mom is steaming. I get up, pick the keys up off the floor. "Hey, I'll trade you for my Mustang."

She half laughs. "I guess it does seem stupid, doesn't it? How many women wouldn't love a new car for Christmas?"

"Sounds like it's the giver, not the gift," I say.

She comes over for a hug. "I would rather he'd gotten me something I wanted."

"What do you want?"

She pulls away. "I don't want *things*, Quin. It's never about *things*."

I don't get it, but she doesn't need to hear that. "He's a dictator."

"I know it seems that way." Mom goes to the Christmas tree, repositions an ornament.

It burns me that she reverts to defensive mode toward him. I already know how he takes control and ruins people's lives. "What would you call him?"

"Spence is a powerful man." She adjusts another ornament. "And powerful men are used to getting their way. He isn't petty, just focused. I was attracted to that once. The power. Now"—she heads for the kitchen—"not so much."

I'm left alone. The tree lights blink. Needles have already begun to fall on the carpet and the perfectly wrapped presents, most still unopened beneath the tree. What I think is that the SUV is gone. The one possible physical link between me and a hit-and-run accident.

And I also wonder if dumping the Caddy was just my father's way of taking out insurance because he doesn't trust me. And hasn't since I was fourteen.

Laurie

DECEMBER 31–JANUARY 2

"I'm telling you, Judie, it was freaky. Here I am standing in Quin's house looking right at Analise's boyfriend. I didn't expect that!"

Judie has just returned from visiting her grandparents in Florida and we're in my room on New Year's Eve, watching TV, waiting for the ball to drop in Times Square. Mom's gone to bed and this is our first chance to talk.

Judie rolls her eyes. "I hope you didn't get that deer-caught-in-the-headlights expression on your face."

"It *rattled* me," I say.

"Because you feel guilty. But you can't let guilt ruin your show."

"Don't psychoanalyze me. I was the one in the car with Quin. Now I know we hit that girl."

" 'We'?" She looks puzzled. "Quin was driving. Where's the 'we' in that? What are you thinking?"

She just doesn't get it. "All I'm telling you is I got a case of the nerves when I saw Jeremy at Quin's house. That's all."

The holidays have been a big boring disappointment for me. Mostly because Mom's been working, Judie's been gone and my dad didn't come like he'd promised. At the last minute, an assignment came up and his editor pressured him to take it, so he did. Mom blew off his no-show, but I really missed seeing him. "I'll come over spring break," he said. "Promise."

Judie asks, "So when does your hotshot boyfriend get back from his family ski trip?"

"Tomorrow."

"And school's on again in two days. So tell me how bad you feel once you start walking down the halls by Quin's side. Once you're the girl of the moment. The one he can't drop. And once baseball season starts, let me know how freaky it is being Quin Palmer's girlfriend then."

I screw up my courage and ask, "Why are you doing this? Why are you helping me get Quin Palmer? We've been friends a long time, but this is hard to understand, Judy. Why?"

"Because I can." Her flip answer doesn't match the look in her eyes, which is solemn.

"Okay. I must ask you. Tell me what do *you* get from this? What do *you* want?"

"I want to be tall, thin, blond and pretty like you. I've always wanted that. I think that's not news to you." The old smart-aleck Judie returns.

I smile. "What else? Be serious."

"I don't like that crowd you want to run with, Laurie. Actually, I'm not blaming you. They think they're so cool. So perfect. I'll never get in— especially because of my looks. But you can. I like knowing that between us we can make them jump through our hoops."

"So you see it as being a puppet master?"

"Something like that. Think of it as a real-life Xbox game." She grins. "I like pushing buttons. Not yours, of course. Quin and his type will never notice me or care about me, but I have the satis- faction of knowing I can make his life miserable. I get secret pleasure out of that. It's a fun sensation even if it is our secret. Don't call me crazy either."

When Quin and I walk into the commons on Janu- ary second, every head turns in our direction. Some of the kids begin to whisper to one another, and it doesn't take a rocket scientist to figure out that some are betting on how long Quin and I will last. I hold the trump card that no one knows about: He won't be dropping me until I say so.

The feeling is delicious, almost sweet. I am startled at how happy it makes me feel. I think of how my mother is not on my back so much and how I've taken control instead of feeling weak and insignificant. Well, I can't deny to myself that I feel just a trace of bitterness because I know how I got here. I shove it out of my mind, move closer to Quin's side, take his hand. I can be tough, why not? He doesn't let go either, but I can feel by his grip that he doesn't like it. *So what?* I am capable of dealing with more than I have ever imagined.

When the bell rings, I give him a kiss on the cheek. I feel his jaw tighten. "See you at lunch," I say, and sashay off to class. I sometimes cannot believe the new me. I am almost transformed. I still am secretly amazed.

Later, passing me in the hall on the way to the cafeteria, Kathy, a girl from the cross-country team, stops me. "So what's with you and Quin and the PDA in the commons? I thought the two of you were over last October."

PDA, shorthand for public display of affection, isn't my usual behavior. I offer what I hope is a coy smile. "Obviously we patched it up."

She looks skeptical. "Make sure he's had his shots. He's done a few girls between last October and now."

I flinch. "Not every girl he dates has sex with him."

"Oh, right. And you're an exception because . . . ?"

I feel my cheeks redden. "Because I tell him no, and I am not as ordinary as you'd imagine."

"Why didn't I think of that?" Kathy says, slapping her forehead. "Oh, don't look so surprised. It was one time only at a party last summer. And just to ease your mind, we used a condom. At least he *knows* how to be careful."

Speechless, I watch her walk away.

· 32 ·

ANALISE

Sometimes when I rise to the surface, I hear Mom reading school lessons to me. I like the sound of her voice. It soothes, like ointment on a burn. My parents are so loyal to this cause of waking me from my coma. I appreciate and admire their determination. Yet I hear what the doctors say. *Three months*. That's kind of a magic number in coma land. Once I've been down for three months, it's unlikely I'll ever emerge. Me. Analise Bower. What remains is a breathing vegetable. *Funny, ha-ha.* I'm little more than a carrot, or an onion. Tubes feed me. Bags hold waste from inside me. Other people care for me. My family, my Jeremy, a friend or two come and watch by my bed. The onion sleeps.

I remember philosophy class again, all the wise and learned men who have tried to explain the unexplainable, who write entire books in an effort to comprehend mankind's existence and our purpose in the universe. I read once in my textbook about a philosopher, Nietzsche, who had become famous for declaring "God is dead." In the margin of the book, someone had written in ink: "Nietzsche is dead. —God." Very funny because it's true. We all die. But I don't want to die. Not yet. Not until I know who did this to me.

I remember my experience in the emergency room. My mind, the essence of me, rising out of my body, floating and watching, going higher, leaving the hospital and entering a tunnel, and a light more beautiful than anything I've ever seen. And I wonder, why can't I float my mind out of this body that cannot move? Why can't I come and go into the world around me without entering the tunnel? How much control do I truly have in mind and matter, over time and space? Can I split myself into parts? Can I break apart like a seedpod and float my consciousness into the real world while my body languishes on this bed?

The idea intrigues me. If I can break free, if I can project myself out of the shell of my body . . . I can go anywhere.

· 33 ·

Quin

I'm walking into the house after indoor practice at the baseball center my dad built a few years ago. Our city had no batting or pitching cages, so Dad bought an old roller rink and had it converted into a facility for Little League and Major League Baseball wannabes to practice to their hearts' content. He also hired a special pitching coach for me, and I've just spent an hour on my technique. I want to ice my arm because I'm really sore, but before I can get through the foyer, Dad calls me into his den. *Now what?*

He's sitting behind his new desk and he's beaming. "Guess who I just got off the phone with?"

God? I shrug.

"A coach from Southern Cal."

Now I'm interested. "And?"

"And he wants to take a look at you. I've planned a little road trip for us over your spring break. We're hitting four California campuses and talking to recruiters there, so keep your pitching arm in shape."

"That's what I've been working on." California! He can't imagine how much I want to go far, far away.

"Of course, several Carolina coaches have been calling, and last week we got a nibble from Nebraska."

"I'd like to go out west."

"It's all about the best offer," Dad says.

We both know that he can afford to send me anywhere, but it's not about scholarship money. It's about playing for the best coaches, the best school, and my best shot at a pro career. The top college players go to farm teams for the big leagues. And that's where I want to be—in Major League Baseball.

I ask, "So we'll spend the whole break making the rounds?" Just yesterday, I told my friends to count me in for a week in Hilton Head and I've already been working on a way to dump Laurie for the trip.

"Is that going to be a problem?"

"No way." I mean it too. I'll miss the beach party, but not the pressure from Laurie. This is my future.

I'm turning to leave when Dad says, "About this girl you're dating . . ."

I freeze. "What about her?"

"Laurie Stark," he says. "You like her?"

"She's all right. Why?"

"It's the second time you've dated her, isn't it?"

My heart's hammering. I could lie, but he wouldn't have asked if he didn't know. "Yeah. We tried dating last fall, but we didn't gel then."

"And now you do?"

"Better than before. I'm just biding my time until graduation. I'm not letting anything get in my way."

He nods, steeples his fingers together, stares hard at me. "You're being careful, though, aren't you?"

More careful than you can imagine, I think. I say, "Remember? I learned my lesson a long time ago."

He smiles grimly. "That was for your own good, Quin. As your father, I only want what's best for you. You can't get off track with some girl. Keep your priorities straight."

My stomach tightens. "My priorities are as straight as an arrow."

"Good. Now go ice your arm."

I take the ice bag to my room, flop down on my bed and allow my mind to go where I rarely let it—to memories of Cory. When she told me she was pregnant, I was scared. But I was glad too. I loved her and wanted to live with her forever. We talked about getting married, even though we were only fourteen. How stupid of me! We were going to run away together, but once Dad found out, he practically locked me in the house.

We had a huge fight over Cory, one I still remember.

"What are you thinking, Quin? Oh, I know what body part you're thinking *with*, but use your head! This girl is a slut."

"No! I love her. Don't call her that."

"Come on, son. Grow up. You're the kid of one of the richest men in the area. You don't think little Miss Trailer Trash sees an opportunity here?"

"Cory's not that way!"

"Well, let's just test your theory, okay?"

And then she was gone. Cory and her whole

family went away, and I know it was my dad's doing. Mr. Ochoa was a poor man, a laborer, and I know my father paid him big bucks to disappear. Later Mom told me that Cory had had an abortion. But I know that Cory was Roman Catholic, and there was no way her family would have aborted our baby. Months later, I ran into one of Cory's old girlfriends, and she told me that Cory was living in Los Angeles and she'd had the baby—a boy—and that her father had forced her to give him up for adoption.

The news made me sad and a little crazy for a time. Somewhere I have a son. Somewhere he's growing up not knowing me. I've made a promise to myself. When I'm a baseball star, when I'm grown and can tell my dad to eat dirt, I'm going to look for my kid.

Today was the closest Dad's come in four years to mentioning this black hole in my life. The last time he talked about it, I was fourteen, Cory was gone and I was confined to my room. He came inside and tossed a large cigar box onto my bed. "This is for you," he said. "I don't ever want to have a scare like this again." And he slammed the door when he left. I stared at the box for a long time, thinking it might contain a snake that would mercifully bite and poison me so I'd never feel this bad again, but when I opened the box I found that it was filled with neat foil packets of condoms. There must have been well over a hundred.

I got his message about girlfriends loud and clear.

· 34 ·

JEREMY

In the barn where Mark keeps his shop, he has a locked room with shelves full of rare woods. I like to go in there to be by myself, to think, and to breathe the sweet air. The scent of the different woods is exotic, heady. I run my hands along the planks of curly maple and cherry, satinwood, quilted mahogany and the rarest of his stash, ebony. I imagine where each came from, their forests and countries, and I wonder if one day I can go to these places and see the trees tall, uncut and raw.

I touch the wood and imagine that I'm touching Analise. Her body was once so beautiful to me. When I lay beside her and looked into her eyes, I saw softness and light, humor and understanding. It's almost impossible to see her in the same way now, curled up on the bed, her hands in splints so they won't turn under, clawlike, her legs drawn up like a newborn baby's. I remember her by Amy's pool, stretched out on a lounge chair, with legs that went on forever, her shimmering veil of hair tied neatly in a ponytail and wound up atop her head, her skin glowing bronze in the sun.

My hands begin to shake. I want her back so much! I want to caress and stroke her, feel desire rise up in me. I want to kiss her, taste her mouth and tongue, fresh with the sour lemon candy she likes to suck. I want to bury my face between her breasts, taste the perspiration on her bronze skin, watch goose bumps rise along her flesh. I want . . . *I want* . . .

The door opens and Mark comes inside. "How you doing, buddy?"

I moisten my lips, turn my back to him because I don't want him to see the tears in my eyes. I clear my throat. "All right. Just looking over the wood."

"Anything new about Analise?" He won't be sidetracked; he knows I come in here when I've got something weighty on my mind.

"Jack told me that the cops have hit a wall with her case. It's gone cold, so they filed it along with all the other cold cases."

"That stinks."

"We'll never know . . . never get justice."

"Closure," Mark says. "That's what the shrinks call it."

That makes me smile because Mark's as far away from armchair psychology as a person can be. "Sure. Closure."

"Come on, we'll lock up and I'll buy you a cup of coffee."

"I've got work—"

"I know the boss. He'll be all right about it." He winks.

I touch the wood once more before leaving the room with Mark. "Did you get Lisa something for Valentine's Day?" Lisa's his wife, and last year we made jewelry boxes for both her and Analise.

"I made her a cedar chest for the foot of our bed. She's been nagging me about one for ages."

This Valentine's Day, I only sat beside Analise's bed and held her hand. Sonya made a cake for the staff and Jack sent a bouquet of red and white balloons. For what? Analise will never know. Her eyes will never see. I shake my head to throw off the heavy dark cloud on my shoulders. I watch Mark lock up the rare woods room. "Promise me something," I say.

"Anything."

"If you ever build anything out of this wood, you'll let me help."

"There aren't many calls for this stuff because it's so expensive, but if I get the chance to build with it, you'll be right by my side."

I'm grateful for that.

· 35 ·

Laurie

I hate baseball. I hate sitting on cold metal bleachers in the cold spring air, cheering for a team I don't care about and a boyfriend I like even less. But if I didn't, people would question my loyalty to the best player on our school's team. Everyone worships Quin. Local reporters are at every game, and his face is a regular on the sports pages.

He's affectionate and caring in public, hateful to me in private. The hypocrite. I'm locked in, though. The coach pulled me aside to talk to me, to send a subtle message. He said, "Nothing throws a player off worse than girlfriend troubles. I sure hope you and Quin can avoid them."

I'd wanted to scream at him, *"You're so wrong! He'd improve a hundred percent if I stopped seeing him."* Instead I smiled and said, "I'm in for the long haul. At least until graduation."

Quin's friends hate me. I know because I walk into a bathroom at school after lunch one day and run into Karen, the girl dating Quin's best friend, Dylan, and certainly the alpha female of the high school's insiders. She and three of her cohorts are sneaking a smoke.

"What's up?" I ask, wearing my biggest smile.

"What's it look like?"

"Aren't you afraid you'll get caught?"

"What are they going to do? Suspend us? Hold off graduation?" Karen takes a drag. "We're seniors. End of May, end of high school game." She looks me over while I smile stupidly. My reflection in the wall mirror reminds me of an eager puppy waiting for approval. "You know what we don't get, Laurie?" she says.

I shrug. Her eyes are glittery and I know that what she has to say isn't going to leave me feeling warm and fuzzy.

"None of us get *you*. And especially what Quin sees in you."

My face goes hot and her blunt words sting. "There's nothing to get. We're just dating."

Karen glances at the others and they look equally malicious. "You don't make him happy. He thinks up ways to *not* be around you. He doesn't even mention you when you're not around. That's just not the way a guy in love treats his girl. So we're wondering . . . why is that?"

I'm speechless. And worse, other girls have come into the bathroom and are listening, standing and watching while the seniors girls diss me. For a moment, I'm afraid I'm going to break down. This isn't working. Being Quin's girl is not the road to popularity I thought it would be. I retreat from the bathroom telling myself I should give up. But I don't.

When I get home one afternoon, Mom's practically dancing around the kitchen.

"Why are you so happy?" I ask. "Big sale?" That's usually what makes her happy—a big commission.

"Oh, my angel! I have the most wonderful news."

Angel? She hasn't called me that since I was ten. "I'm listening."

She dances over and cups my face in her hands, giving my cheeks a squeeze. "I owe it all to you."

"Me?" I figure Mom's finally lost it. Dating Quin Palmer for a few months has not magically turned me into Lindsey Duvales.

"Guess who's been offered the job as marketing manager for Spencer Palmer's newest housing development?"

I get a funny fluttering feeling in my stomach. "You?"

"Don't sound so skeptical. Yes, me! I'll be on staff and bringing home a huge salary." She leans closer. "So much more money that I can buy you a car of your own. How's that sound?"

I'd really like my own car, especially because I've been riding the bus since I turned sixteen in January. Now that I'm eating lunch with Quin's crowd, Judie's found new friends and hasn't been picking me up for school. We don't hang together much either these days. "I don't need a car."

She gives me a surprised look. "But you want one, don't you?"

I ignore her question and ask, "But what about your real estate office? I thought you work for Treasured Homes."

"*Worked* for," she says. "I quit today. As soon as I walked in from having lunch with Spencer."

"B-but you can't!"

"Why ever not? Laurie, I thought you'd be happy for me. For us. This is a huge career step up."

My brain's in a tailspin. Mom working for

Quin's dad! I've run into the man at his house and at the ball field, but we've never had a conversation. "Tell me about the job," I say.

"He called me out of the blue and invited me to lunch and offered me the job. Told me he remembers how I hustled and sold homes in his other divisions. He said he's been watching my work grow and mature. For crying out loud, Laurie, I've arrived! Let's show some enthusiasm."

"But I date Quin."

"Of course you do."

"What happens if . . . when we break up?"

Mom pats my shoulder. "Give me some credit here. I think Spencer did take more notice of me because of your relationship with Quin, but I'm a good worker, and I deserve this break."

She's getting upset and I sure don't need that. I drop the books still clutched in my arms and grab her in a hug. "I'm sorry. I—I wasn't thinking. You do deserve this, and you'll be great at the job."

She pulls away. "That's better." She flashes a smile and her eyes light up. "Of course, we must celebrate. Dinner at our favorite place?" Before I can say anything, she adds, "That is, if you don't have other plans with Quin."

I shake my head. "Not tonight."

"Then let's change. Let's wear pretty clothes. Something springlike."

I watch her dash from the room, leaving me to feel like I'm being sucked into a tornado.

· 36 ·

Quin
MARCH 1–15

Sometimes when I see Laurie sitting in the bleachers pretending to cheer for me, I want to pop a fly ball her way in hopes of knocking her out. I tell myself, *Just another couple of months and she's history*. Once spring break's over and I'm back from California, it's only another six weeks until I graduate. I'm making certain she doesn't welsh on our deal to break up with me by leaving for baseball camp two days after graduation. Dad's arranged everything. I intend to leave little Laurie in the dust.

What I can't stand is the way she lords it over me when we're with my friends. She hangs on my arm. She giggles and cuddles next to me when we're out with others. When we're alone, it's a different story. She won't let me touch her. Not that I want to. Not anymore. If she walked in front of me naked, begging me to have sex with her, I'd walk away. That's how much I don't like her.

I could tell Dad. But I won't. I couldn't stand him having something else to rub my nose in, the way he did about Cory. I can hear him say, *"Screwed up again? What's with you, boy? Do I have to clean up every mess you make?"* He doesn't need to know that Laurie was in the car that night I hit a deer that was most likely not a deer, but Analise Bower, whom the school still treats like a saint. Her best friend is even holding pages open in the yearbook for a tribute!

So I endure Laurie and questions from my friends about why I'm dating her, and what I see in the little drip. I'm thinking that if I make her miserable enough, she'll call off the deal. Wouldn't that be sweet?

One night I'm watching a cop show on TV and the story line is about blackmail. That's what Laurie's doing. She's blackmailing me. And then one of the characters says something that opens a door for me. *Insight. Understanding.* I do some research on the Web, get the details straight. I don't have to just sit still and take Laurie's crap anymore. I can strike back, make her run scared too.

We go to a movie with Karen and Dylan on

Saturday night. Laurie's all lovey-dovey until my friends split in the parking lot and Laurie and I are alone in my car. She moves to the far side of her bucket seat, treats me like I've become a leper. Before I crank the engine, I say, "You know, Laurie, I've been thinking about the night of the accident."

I see her stiffen. "What about it?"

"Maybe you're wrong."

"I've heard that the police have closed the investigation. If I say something, they'll open it again."

I want to wipe that smugness out of her voice. "You realize that if you do, you'll be implicated too."

"No way. I was just a passenger."

"But you knew about it. You've known about it for months. And you've never said a word."

"So?"

She's looking hard at me now and I return her look, move in for the kill.

"So in the land of law and order, you'd be called an accessory. That's someone who helps someone else commit a crime. It's a criminal offense."

"I didn't help you!"

My pent-up venom gushes out. "You were

there. You never came forward. You've helped me hide it all this time. Oh, you're guilty, all right. Guilty as if you were driving the car. You think about that."

The shocked look on her face is worth a million bucks. I start the engine and drive her home.

· 37 ·

ANALISE
FEBRUARY 1–MARCH 15

In my dreams, I fly.

Do doctors know that coma patients dream? Perhaps I'll tell them when I wake up. I love my dream state, am amazed and rewarded whenever I achieve it. At first, the scenes I visit are from my past. Memories flow like a steady stream of water. I see me younger, Mom and Dad holding my hand, taking me places. . . . Disney World when I was seven and Washington, D.C., when I was ten. I see Amy, and I watch us growing up. I see Jeremy and watch us growing together. I taste our first kiss. I see the high school, the halls full of kids, walking, chattering, believing that these days must be hurried through. I long to meld into the stream heading to classes.

I don't know when I realize that I can control my flights into memory, but one night, I sense a shift. I no longer stare into the past. I float upward and look down and I see my body on the bed, as if I'm hovering over myself. I see what I have become. Not Analise. Not the girl in my memories. I look grotesque. I feel sorry for me. Then one night my consciousness rises out of my body, soars through the confinement of my room, sends me out into the night. Like a vampire, I seek blood. Not literally, of course, but metaphorically. I want to find the person who did this to me.

As I soar, I am aware that a flesh-and-blood body is a cumbersome thing. It moves with difficulty, like a machine from another age run with pulleys and rubber bands. I realize that the human body is hard to manipulate and is bound by gravity. No wonder it takes babies and children years to control these inferior vessels. Not so with my consciousness. I float freely through time and space, unhampered by walls. I am spirit instead of flesh and bone. Perhaps God gave us bodies so that we are forced to slow down, although I can't imagine why. If only I could tell the people I love that I'm here, above their world, in their space, but not visible to them. *I think, therefore I am.* Did Descartes form his philosophy because he too could send his consciousness into the invisible world?

Each time I drift out of my body, my mind

grows stronger while my body grows weaker. I sense my life force draining away. The doctors check me, but they don't sense the weakness stealing over my flesh, too subtle, I suspect, for their instruments to pick up. No matter. When I'm free-floating, I feel invincible.

The only downside of my freedom is how sensitive it makes me to the thoughts and emotions of others. I sense people's joy, pain, anger, fear—a spectrum of human feelings that leaves me confused, exhausted. The mental storms bombard me, strike like misfiring electrons that snap and crackle and crowd out my presence. The energy waves of others toss me back into the body on the bed and into the realm of coma. Here I, Analise Bower, disappear until, through strength of will and the magic of dreams, I again break free to visit the world of the living, of those trapped inside physical bodies and locked in time.

· 38 ·

Laurie
APRIL 4–9

"Hi, Daddy!" I throw myself into my father's arms the second he opens the door of his hotel room.

"Wow! This is some greeting, baby girl."

I bury my face in his chest and I want to cry, but I stop myself. Too much explaining if I do.

"Let me take a good look at you, Laurie. It's been so long. I'm really sorry I couldn't get here over Christmas." He holds me at arm's length and looks me over. His smile fades a bit. "You look beautiful—just thin. You're not on one of those crazy teenage diets, are you? Because you shouldn't be."

I assure him I'm not.

"Good, then let's go to lunch." He grabs his jacket.

I'm not hungry. All I want to do is curl up on the sofa and be Daddy's little girl. "All right."

"You can show me that new car of yours."

"It's not so new," I tell him as we go down in the elevator.

"Man, I remember my first car—a Dodge Charger, red with chrome wheels, black leather interior. I restored it myself. Sure wish I'd hung on to it. It would be worth a fortune today."

Outside, the signs of spring are everywhere. Daffodils are thick in the beds in front of the hotel, and cherry trees are bursting with pink blossoms along the downtown street. The sun's bright, the air is cold and I shiver. I lead Dad to my car, parked down the street. He walks around the older-model blue Honda Civic, patting the hood and trunk, kicking the tires and peering inside at the gray interior. "Your mother chose well. She must be doing great."

I see sadness in his eyes and I know he's wishing he could have bought me my first car. I hook my arm through his. "It's just a car, Dad."

"It's every teen's dream. It's freedom," he says. Well, at least he got one right.

If only I *was* free. But I have no liberty. Quin's revelation about my accessory status hangs over my head and haunts me day and night. I've gone online and researched what he's told me and I've discovered that he's right. I'm as guilty as he because

I said and did nothing! All these months, I was fixated on my own agenda, on elevating my own popularity and dealing with my mother's expectations. But it's been a bust. The guilt over Analise and what we've done is eating me up.

If I see Jeremy in the halls, I duck into the closest room, or—like the other day when I unknowingly parked beside him in the student lot at school—I take off in the opposite direction like a rabbit. The school grapevine hardly mentions Analise anymore, except for Amy collecting wishes from students for the upcoming yearbook. I swear I'm not even buying one of the books. This is one year I want to forget!

Nothing's turned out the way I wanted. My life's in the toilet. I can't talk about it with anyone, not even Judie, who appears to have forgotten we were in this together. I corner her one afternoon in the parking lot and I say, "You never call anymore."

"The phone works both ways."

Her rebuke stings. "I—I've just been crazy busy trying to keep all the balls in the air. I thought you were going to become my chief advisor. What about being puppet master and Xbox controller?"

She gives me a cool glance. "You haven't consulted me in weeks. Since we have such different schedules, and friends, Laurie, you are not part of my life anymore."

Is that true? She looks hurt, and I think about seeing her with a new crowd sitting at the lunch tables, "commoners," according to Karen and her group. I had laughed with them, and Karen had asked meanly, "Isn't the fat one a friend of yours, Laurie?"

My cheeks burned. "I—I know her. Since elementary school."

"She not only needs to lose weight, she dresses in clothes no one should wear. You should dump her," Karen said.

"I have," I snapped, then instantly regretted saying it.

Now, facing Judie, I know I've let her down majorly. How had things gotten so out of control? "Maybe we can hit the mall on Saturday."

She studies me. "You don't want to be seen anywhere with me. We both know that." She doesn't sound sarcastic, just sad. "I don't know why I didn't predict this. It's like a bad teen movie, I've seen it a hundred times, but I thought you'd be different."

"No. Really."

Judie holds up her hand. "Please, don't. We've both moved on, Laurie. I gave you what you wanted—a way to be popular and get your mother off your case. Don't worry about me. You've got enough other real stuff to worry about. I'm surprised at both of us, really."

Her words hurt. Yet she's the only person who knows the truth. What if she turns on me?

She seems to read my mind. She takes a step back. "Your secret's safe with me. Who would believe we'd come up with the idea of, well, blackmail? No one. Don't get nervous on my account. I think Quin's waiting for you over there."

I look across the lot behind me and sure enough, Quin's glaring at us from beside his truck. "I—I have to go," I say to Judie.

"Sure you do." She clutches her books to her chest and turns.

I want to call to her to come back, but my tongue feels stuck to the roof of my mouth. Quin's car horn blows and I hurry to him, all the time telling myself that Judie wants out of this mess and is doing what's best for her, not me. I can hardly believe after all our years of friendship that it has come to this—but I know it is over, and I am someone else now.

Dad takes me to a small restaurant and we buy gourmet hamburgers. I have to choke mine down because he's watching me through every bite.

When we're finished, he volunteers to take me to buy a new spring outfit, but I beg off, tell him I want to go back to his hotel and veg out. Once there, he pours me a cola and makes small talk about his job and a woman he's begun to date. I say, "Maybe I can meet her this summer when I come over."

"I'd like that." He fiddles with a sofa pillow. "Laurie, is something bothering you?"

I shrug. "High school's hard. Not at all the fun thrill Mom keeps telling me it was for her. She expects so much for me."

"Your mom was the most popular girl in school, so it was fun for her. She got to call the shots. That's not true for everyone."

"So power's the key?"

"Not power. Attitude. If you want a friend, be a friend. She was outgoing and totally unbiased about who she hung with. People liked her in spite of not wanting to like her. I sure fell hard." He smiles. "I felt like the luckiest guy in the world when she chose me."

His words only underline the differences between Mom and me. "Well, these days, guys run the show."

His brow knits. "This guy you're dating, he's not . . . you know . . . not pressuring you, is he?

Not asking you for things you don't want to give him? Because if he is—"

"No, Dad," I interrupt. "Nothing's going on between me and Quin . . . like you're asking about." I squirm. If only it *was* something as simple as being pressured for sex. I want to talk about my predicament without giving myself away, and ponder how to do it. I decide that I should act studious, be a seeker of information.

"I—um, well, you're a reporter. What if you know something that would hurt a lot of people if you told it? It's for a paper I'm writing," I add hastily. "Hypothetical."

He takes a while to answer, and when he does, he holds my hand. "As a reporter, I try to consider the greater good, not just the issue and the people involved. You hear that journalists break a story using the defense that the public has a right to know. In truth, the public doesn't give a flip about most stuff. The public is often clueless and uninterested until newshounds make them interested. So before I break a big story—and I've only broken two in my career—I weigh the consequences."

He pauses, looks at me. "Too much information?"

I shake my head.

"You sure this is just about a paper?"

Heat skitters up my cheeks. "Of course, Dad."

He tousles my hair, looks serious again. "On the other hand, sometimes a person just has to do the right thing. No matter what the consequences. And that's a question for your heart, not your brain. Journalists have a moral obligation—well, every citizen does. You understand this."

Doing *the right thing* will change a lot of lives forever. And it will make my father hate me.

I'm parked in front of the long-term care facility where Analise is living. I don't even remember driving here. I just look up and here I am. My heart is pounding and my mouth is dry. I tell myself to drive away, not to get out and go inside. I lose the battle with myself. I guess I've known for a long time now that I have to see her.

At the reception station, I almost chicken out. *What am I thinking?* These places have security. People can't just walk in off the street and expect to be allowed in. Behind the desk, an older woman is on duty, and I tell her who I'm here to see. She confesses that the regular receptionist is out sick, that she's a temp, but that she knows only certain visitors are allowed in Ms. Bower's room. She picks up a clipboard. "Your name?"

"Amy Cartwright." I lie—something I'm getting very good at these days.

"Yes . . . here you are." She smiles and hands me a visitor's tag.

"I—it's been a while since I've visited. I'm sorry, but I don't remember her room number."

She tells me and I hurry off, checking numbers beside open doors and hoping no one will stop me. When I find Analise's room, I stop to catch my breath. I can't slow my racing heart. My feet feel heavy, and it takes all my courage to step inside the room.

· 39 ·

ANALISE

Someone's in my room that I don't know. Occasionally a new nurse will come in, but I sense that this person isn't part of the medical staff. I know because this person is afraid. I smell the fear. Over time, I've learned to filter the emotions of others so as not to be overwhelmed by them. The girl in my room is full of emotion, but fear is the one that washes over me, like a light turned on in darkness.

Tentatively I reach out to better know her. I sense her, but she can't sense me. Only those closest to me seem to feel when I'm present, when my mind is alert and aware. But this girl is a stranger. And she's crying. Am I so hideous? The ones who love me see me through different eyes, but strangers, well, they see me as I am . . . a body curled on a bed, with eyes that open wide, close, flutter, but see nothing. All that I "see," all that I know, I gather with my mind, the conscious part of me, which I'm learning to control.

I wonder if she'll come closer to the bed. She doesn't. Slowly her fear morphs into pity, and after pity, remorse. How odd. Why remorse? I soak my consciousness into hers and am astounded. She's had a car accident. No. She has knowledge of a car accident. She has knowledge of *my* accident! The revelation hurls me backward, as if I'd hit a wall and bounced. She knows something! Why has she come? To check me out? To see for herself that her secret is forever safe because I'm in a coma?

Her emotions are raw, yet also tender. I want to speak to her, ask her questions. I have no voice. I have no hands to reach out and take hold of her. And I'm slipping away too. Oozing back into the nowhere place where I sleep when my consciousness can no longer assert itself.

My body thrashes on the bed and the girl stifles a scream and flees from the room.

Again I am alone. And my enemy is free.

· 40 ·

Quin

This has been the best week of my life. And for the first time, I feel that I can do no wrong in my old man's eyes. He's proud of me! I never thought I'd see the day. Every campus we visited, every coach we talked to, was better than the one before. They want me, all of them, and just because I can throw a baseball. We're on the plane, flying back to Asheville after a layover in Atlanta from the West Coast.

"I like Southern Cal and UCLA," I say, not that he asked my opinion.

"No decisions until your offers from the Carolinas come in."

I want to leave the Carolinas, but I know this isn't the time to make my case. "I still have to finish out the high school year."

"I'm not sure you should. What if you get injured? No need for you to take too many risks with your arm. This is just high school. You've got years of games ahead of you."

I panic. Playing ball is the only reason I get up and go to school every day. "I can't let Coach and the team down," I say. "We have a shot at State. It would be nice to win that. It'll look good on my resume." I'm smart enough to use his lingo.

He looks thoughtful. "It would be nice. I'll talk to your coach. Maybe you can play, just not too much."

I feel like I've dodged a bullet.

"Want a beer?" Dad asks.

"You'd let me have one?"

"Come on, son. It's not like I don't know you drink the stuff." He takes a sip of his second bourbon and water since takeoff. "The trick," he continues, "is to know how to hold your liquor. And to not do stupid things when you drink."

My stomach knots. *What's he saying?* "Such as?"

"Oh, I don't know . . . maybe like racking up your mother's new car by hitting a deer."

The way he says it turns my blood ice-cold. Laurie wouldn't have said anything to him, would she? "It was an accident," I say, wishing I had his bourbon.

He looks at me hard, like he's weighing just

how much to say, like he's waiting for me to spill my guts about the night of the accident. Like I won't.

"According to the body shop where I took the car, the deer had green paint on it."

I feel like heaving, but I keep silent. Finally I say, "There were a lot of cars parked all over the yard at the party. One probably backed into Mom's. It was dark. I didn't look for damage before I drove off."

His gaze is steady and I hold it, knowing I can't crack. He nods slowly. "I guess it could have happened that way."

We stare at each other for a few more seconds, and I realize that something has been settled between us. "I'll take that beer now," I say.

He asks the stewardess for a beer, leans back against the headrest.

He takes the beer and she walks away. He gives it to me. I sip it, dreading getting home and returning to my real life. And to Laurie.

At least she didn't call me over spring break. The week apart has made me downright cheerful. How did I ever get into this? It had never crossed my mind that a girl like that could be so awful. I notice a pretty woman two rows up and across the aisle. It's nice to be able to look at another female without Laurie going ballistic—just for show, and we both know it. But it's made me paranoid. I half expect Laurie to lean around the seat in front of mine and say, *"Thinking of cheating, Quin? Don't!"*

Why did I let that girl get so into my life? She was just another nothing to me. How could I know? If she opens her big mouth, college, baseball, my dad's approval rating—all of it's over. I sure didn't mean to hit that girl on her bike. I didn't even know it until—well, later. And maybe I should have told Dad a long time ago, but I didn't. Only a few more months and I can put this nightmare behind me.

"You still dating Laurie?"

His question catches me off guard. Is he reading my mind? "Sure."

"But you're willing to give her up when the time comes?"

"As soon as camp starts."

"And she's good with that?"

"She's known all along that I have other plans for my life." My palms are sweating, so I set the beer down, afraid I'll drop it. "Nothing's going to get in my way, Dad."

He nods, looking satisfied with my answers. "She has calmed you down a lot; I'll give her that much."

"She doesn't like to party," I say, in an effort to explain my changed behavior.

"You might want to remember that once you get to college."

"I'll remember," I say, seeing that he's in lecture mode. I know to be agreeable. The week's been too good to mess it up with an argument this close to home.

"Plus there are rules for athletes on scholarship. All the coaches we met were forthright about that."

"I'll behave." All I want is *out of here*.

A baby begins to cry somewhere behind us. Dad groans. "I hope someone shuts up that kid. I sure don't want to listen to some screaming brat for another hour."

I slouch in my seat, think again of my son. He would be close to three by now. I wonder who's raising him. I can hardly believe what happened to me back then. I don't know if I loathe myself or my dad more. I guess myself. I hate this kind of thinking.

I shut off my brain. I finish my beer in one long gulp, slouch in my seat and pull the bill of my ball cap low over my eyes. I pretend to fall asleep while I listen to the crying baby. I'm through talking to my dad, having him dig through my life like a dog looking for a bone. It's never been easy with him. Finally this week is making a difference. I do not want to screw it up. I know I have an approval addiction, but no one is going to get in my way, especially not a blackmailing rat like Laurie. She can't control me forever.

JEREMY

April 28

"Her doctor says she has pneumonia."

Sonya meets me in the hall with a worried look. I stop in my tracks, feeling like the wind's been knocked out of me. "Can't they give her antibiotics?"

"It's viral, so antibiotics won't help. She's really sick, Jeremy."

"Can I still see her?"

Sonya hands me a mask. "You'll have to wear this in the room."

I slip the green mask over my nose and mouth and feel claustrophobic. In the room, Analise is covered by an oxygen mask, and signs announce CAUTION! OXYGEN IN USE. FLAMMABLE! She looks pale and small against the white bedsheets. I take her hand, still curled, clawlike. "Hi, baby."

Standing on the other side of the bed, Sonya

says, "They're going to send her back over to the hospital. They had to take her off the blood thinners, so she's susceptible to more problems."

I nod, unable to speak. Her going back to the hospital underscores just how sick she must be.

Sonya says, "Look, I'll leave you two alone."

I nod again and she slips out of the room, closing the door behind her. Still holding Analise's hand, I ease onto the bed. I like being alone with Analise. I can talk to her freely this way. I tell her everything in my heart, and I know she hears me. "I'm sorry you're sick," I say. "But the docs will fix you up." I press my lips to her hand and force myself to be upbeat. "Mark's got a ton of work, and I spend all my free time at his workshop. I wish you could see some of my projects. He wants me to go to community college in the fall and get some business credits. Says that's his weak spot, that he never got into the business and accounting parts, and that if I learn that stuff, maybe I can partner with him someday. I like the idea, because I don't want to live anywhere else except near you. I mean, you'll be out of this coma someday."

The room is quiet. Sunlight slants through a window and casts my shadow across her body. I want to hold her. "Prom's next week," I say. "I thought we'd be going. But I guess not. Amy's got a hot date with some guy she's been chasing—make that stalking—half the year." I laugh at my own joke. "She says I can come with them, since she knows I won't take anyone but you. Like I care about the stupid prom."

My parents suggested that maybe I should consider moving on with my life. It made me so mad that I didn't speak to them for days. Mom made peace by going on a baking rampage, making all my favorites, and issuing a big-time apology. "Mom's got a ton of relatives coming for graduation," I say. "Including Aunt Betty. You remember her—the nutty one who spends her life on cruise ships instead of renting an apartment." I grin, remembering how much fun Analise and I had talking about the old girl and her many ex-husbands.

Memories of happy times pour through me, and the desire to hold Analise makes my heart ache. I lift up the bedsheet, slide onto the bed behind her, and gently put my arms around her. She barely fills them up, but she's warm, and with her body pressed against me I feel at peace. Her hair has grown out a few inches. It's as soft as down against my nose and lips. I kiss her neck. If anyone walks in on us, I'll probably be banned for life from the place, but I don't care. I only want my arms around her. For a moment, I swear that her body relaxes. It's an illusion, I know, but still, it makes me crazy happy.

· 42 ·

Laurie

APRIL 29

"You don't seem that sick to me," Mom says. "Not sick enough to miss the prom with Quin."

I'm sitting on the sofa in my robe, a box of tissues in my lap, trying to watch some DVD. The tissue box is a prop and so is the robe. I'm not sick in the way I told Mom I was sick. I'm sick in my heart and soul. "There'll be other proms," I tell her, hoping she'll go away.

"Honestly, Laurie, I just don't understand you sometimes. I would have carried my sickbed to the prom in my day."

She's not letting up. "It's just a dance, really," I say. "Don't get carried away."

"It's at the country club. Spencer's reserved the entire place for the senior prom tonight. And what about that beautiful dress we bought you?"

Mom says "Spencer" like they're best friends, and I want to gag. She dragged me into every store downtown until she found the "perfect dress," which I hate. "You can take it back. I never cut off the tags."

"Did you and Quin have a fight?"

I grit my teeth. "I don't feel good, Mom. I'm trying to be responsible here. To not make others sick."

"Well, it's not right that you're making him miss his senior prom, you know."

"I gave him permission to go without me." He was downright gleeful when I told him to go without me.

"But you're his girlfriend! You don't want a guy like Quin footloose. Some girl will snake him away."

"I don't care!" I throw the tissue box across the room. "Don't you get it? I'm not really his girlfriend."

"But you are. He chose you. You're a lovely girl with the hottest guy in school. The perfect high school couple."

I clamp my hands over my ears. "Stop it. Stop talking about me and Quin."

She looks confused, and suddenly the dam behind my eyes breaks. Words bubble up like a geyser. I can no longer live with the lies. No matter what, I must confess to my mother. I spend the next fifteen minutes spewing out my pent-up guilt. I tell her everything. I watch her face go from shocked to horrified to pasty sick. I watch her recoil. I've turned into a freak. Her precious little Laurie is a screwup. She is realizing that her baby had to blackmail her way into popularity by sacrificing justice. An innocent girl is in a coma. *Welcome to my world, Mom!*

Once I'm through spewing, she is silent for a few minutes. Then she looks right at me and asks, "What are you going to do?" Her voice quavers.

I was hoping you'd tell me, I think, but I say, "I don't know."

She stands very still. "A lot of people will be hurt if you say anything."

"I know."

"There would be a lot of loss, Laurie."

For instance, your job, I think, but I just say, "I know."

"Telling won't fix this girl. It won't change her medical condition."

"I know," I repeat.

"And . . . and I'm thinking about you. What's going to happen to you? You're my child. You've got your whole life ahead of you."

Until now, all I've done is think about me. I feel sick, like I'm going to throw up. "I know."

"This can ruin yours and Quin's lives."

"What about *her* life? I think about Analise all the time. I can't get her out of my head."

"But you said it was an accident. No one can blame you and Quin for an accident."

"We should have come forward once we realized what happened."

"You said you didn't know that you'd actually hit a person. That still may be true."

"I know we hit her, Mom. Trust me. I know, and he knows too. Quin knows."

We look at each other, Mom and me, across the distance of the family room. The few feet that separate us feel like a hundred miles. I want her to tell me that everything is going to be all right . . . just fine . . . no need to worry. I want her to say, "Let me handle it." Instead, a mask slips over her face, and her eyes grow cool and distant. She says, "Think hard and long before you speak out, Laurie, before you open this can of worms." I look at her and see an expression I do not like. "I'll have to hire a lawyer, so let me know what you're going to do before you do it." She stops talking then. She almost leaves the room, then turns at the last moment. "I'll support whatever decision you make, but confessing won't be a cure-all. All it will do is create new problems. Remember, you and Quin are young, and so much can happen."

She leaves, and I sit and stare at the empty doorway, feeling shell-shocked. I don't know what I expected her to do, but it wasn't to walk away. I want her to come back, but she doesn't. The sound of silence is heavy, like a smothering blanket. Finally I hear water running upstairs. She's getting ready to go to bed. "Thanks, Mom," I say aloud. "I will have to do this alone." Once again, I outline my choices: speak out or stay silent. I've tried it one way for months. Sure, I got popular, but I feel awful. It hasn't worked.

Tears make the walls blurry. I am alone. I have no friends, no one to care about me. We were a family once—me, Dad and Mom. Then Dad left and it was me and Mom. Now Mom's disappointed and even distant. She's left me too. My whole body aches, like someone's been throwing rocks at me and every missile has scored a direct hit. I almost envy Analise in her coma, at peace, oblivious to the pain and hurt of real life. Maybe it would be best for all if I checked out too. I'm not pitying myself, really, because all I can think is *Who will really miss me?*

· 43 ·

JEREMY

Analise is back in the hospital. She's in an oxygen tent, being given all kinds of meds through IVs. Sonya tells me, "I think she's getting better."

Jack looks tired, like he's run a marathon. They stand with their arms around each other in the waiting area of the ICU. "My poor little girl. She's been through so much."

"Will she go back to the care unit when she's better?" I ask.

Jack and Sonya trade glances. "Actually," Jack says, "we're planning on taking her home once she's out of the woods. We can hire a home-care nurse and a physical therapist to come to the house. Sonya knows how to clean and maintain the feeding tube. I've talked to a contractor, and we're starting renovations on our sunroom come Monday. We'll turn it into a nice permanent-care room for her. And the hospital is only minutes away by ambulance if we run into problems."

I like the idea. "Once she's home, maybe she'll wake up."

"My thoughts exactly," Sonya says.

She smiles, and for the first time in months, I see hope on both their faces.

At two o'clock in the morning, my cell starts singing the "Hallelujah Chorus," and I sit bolt upright in bed. My heart pounds and my blood turns cold. *Analise?* How can she be calling me? Did she wake up? Then I remember that I assigned her ringtone to Sonya and Jack's phone.

I scramble out of bed, stub my toe and curse, stumble to my desk and sweep the top until I feel my phone. I flip it open and manage to croak, "Hello."

Sonya's crying. My heart almost stops. "I—I can't understand you," I say.

I hear the phone being taken over and then Jack's voice. "Analise developed a blood clot. It lodged in her heart."

"B-but how?" I'm confused and my brain's still

fuzzy. I recall that her doctors have taken her off her blood thinners.

Jack's voice says, "She died, Jeremy. Just minutes ago, while we were standing next to her bed, our little girl died."

· 44 ·

Laurie

At two o'clock in the morning, the whole world seems dead. The house is quiet, like a tomb, my room as silent as a grave. Mom's gone to bed and I'm alone and feeling dead. *Serves you right, Laurie Stark.* I haven't felt alive for months. I know now what I have to do. I should have done it a long time ago. It's the only way to turn off the hurt inside me and set things right.

I sit at my computer, wait for words to come. When they come, I write, the clicking of the keys the only sound in the world. My fingers have a life of their own as they follow the script in my head, and the words spill onto the screen in neat little rows.

I will be reviled for what I'm about to do. I am destroying a sports god, a definite no-no in the hallowed halls of Southern high school culture. I'm destroying myself too. But no one will care about that. I must do this if I'm ever going to be free, if I'm ever going to feel clean.

I go to my closet, rummage through a pile of old clothes in the back, where I've hidden a manila folder in an old notebook from the eighth grade. I take it to my desk, where I carefully copy information into the story lengthening on my computer screen. It's the name of the body shop in Charlotte where Quin's dad took the Cadillac SUV to be repaired. Before he dumped it. Before he bought a new Lexus. There are four photos of the damaged fender from different angles, the tell-tale green paint from Analise's bike embedded in the gouges. I scan the photos into my photo software program and attach the file to the e-mail. This is my trump card, my ace in the hole, as I've known it would be. As I planned.

I think back to the day I stole the information. I was in Quin's house and we had a fight. He stormed out, leaving me there. His father was at work, his mom was passed out upstairs and I was alone, fuming, eager for a way to get even with Quin. I marched into his father's den and over to the huge new desk. The top gleamed, smooth as glass, beautiful to see and touch, made in part, I knew, by Jeremy's hands. I went through the drawers, not even sure what I was looking for, just searching for something, anything that would make Quin faithful to his promise to stay with me until I let him go.

Quin's dad hadn't bothered to lock the desk—his bad. His files were neat and alphabetized and well labeled. The one innocently marked CADDY was where I discovered the information about the SUV. The fix-it shop had dutifully filled out the paperwork in every detail. There was a copy machine in the den, so I made a copy, placed it in the file folder, and kept the original along with the photos. I shut the drawer, wiped the top of the desk with the tail of my shirt until it shone, and left the den.

I complete my e-mail message to Amy, yearbook editor at Asheville High School, read and reread it until I know it by heart. It will become the final and most important message in her tribute pages for Analise Bower. I put the cursor on Send, knowing that once I hit the button, there's no turning back. I think about Dad, wonder if he'd approve of what I'm doing, of the story I'm breaking—and if he'll still love me when the truth comes out. I set my finger on the mouse, close my eyes and whisper, "Just do it."

And I click.

· 45 ·

ANALISE

APRIL 30

At two o'clock in the morning, I float freely above my body as it lies on the hospital bed. I simply lift off like a feather drifting on a summer breeze, hovering briefly above the narrow bed, the machines and the medical personnel. I look down on myself, but I feel no more pity. The body on the bed looks vacated, empty, abandoned like a cracked eggshell. I see my parents holding on to each other and crying. I want to tell them I'm fine . . . more than fine. I'm free!

I drift out of the hospital into the night, no longer a captive of time, nor of coma. As I float, I pass my school, my neighborhood, my home. I see through walls as if they were made of clear glass. I see my friends having a sleepover at Amy's. I see a girl hunched over a computer keyboard. I don't know her, and yet she's somehow familiar. *No matter.* My ties to this earth are severed and all I feel is weightlessness and peace. Even when I pass over Jeremy's house, see into his room, see him on his bed, his face buried in his pillow, and know that he's crying, I feel no sadness. I know he loved me and I loved him. There was a time when all I wanted was to be with him. It's different now. Longing and bitterness, fear and anger, malice and vengefulness have all melted away.

The importance of my old life is dimming as I move toward the bright light I've seen once before. It's allowing me to come to it, and this time, I won't be sent back. If only the people I'm leaving behind could understand! There is no sadness where I'm going. Only joy.

I reach out and embrace the light.

JEREMY

MAY 3, 4:00 PM

"How's it coming?" Mark asks.

"I'm almost finished," I tell him. I've been hand-rubbing a coat of beeswax on the coffin we've built for Analise from the rare woods in his workshop. Building it was my suggestion. Using the beautiful woods was Mark's. It was his gift—to me and to her and her family.

Rudy has showed up out of the blue. He said, "Heard about your girl. Real sorry, son. Can I help?"

For three days, we work together on the box that will hold her body. It's a work of art, with sides of curly cherry and a top of quilted mahogany, inlaid with crosses of ebony and bird's-eye maple. I've applied ten layers of wax, rubbing each coat until the wood glows. I let one coat dry, add another, and do it all over again. My back and shoulders throb, my hands ache.

Sonya and Jack came yesterday and lined the inside with foam and pale lavender satin. All that remains is to affix the wooden plaque Amy has prepared, with words she meticulously burned into the grain. Analise will be buried tomorrow in the most beautiful coffin our human hands could make, for all eternity.

Mark says, "I heard that the cops arrested Spence Palmer and charged him as an accessory."

The story was all over the news. The big man on campus, Quin Palmer, had committed the crime, but his father had tried to cover it up by repairing and then dumping the car that hit Analise. The local DA swears he will prosecute. But I know that Spencer Palmer is one of the most powerful men in the state and that Palmer money may slow down justice. "We'll see," I say.

Mark says, "It took guts for Quin's girlfriend to blow the whistle."

I picture Laurie all teary-eyed for the news cameras. "Too little, too late." I have trouble talking about it. Sonya and Jack have found some peace, but if I ever get my hands on Quin, I might kill him.

"Still, it was a brave thing she did, sending that e-mail and those photos to Amy and implicating herself. Did you know her?"

"Not personally. I've seen her around school. She's one of the in-crowd because she was dating Quin. I don't know if she always was." I keep buffing the wood. The cops found the SUV in Pennsylvania, owned by a man who innocently bought it from a car wholesaler in Charlotte. The right fender and bumper were new, but the vehicle ID number matched the one Palmer once owned. The tires were the same too. The right front tread perfectly matched the cast that police forensics had made of a tire mark on the road near the broken guardrail on the night Analise was struck. Quin swore to the police that he thought he'd hit a deer, but I think his story stinks. At some point, according to Laurie, he knew, and he did nothing.

"If you're finished, I'll get my pickup," Mark says.

We're going to drive the coffin to the funeral home, where Analise's body has been prepared for tomorrow's funeral. I step back, look over the box. The finish is flawless. "It's ready."

He leaves, and I know he'll take his time so that I can be alone for a little while. One last thing to do. I pick up the plaque and a drill. I attach the piece of wood to the top, just under the crosses, with tiny brass screws. When the drill stops, quiet comes. I see days without Analise stretching in front of me. When she was in the coma, at least I could see and touch her. Now I can't. This is the hardest part for me.

The air in the old barn is still and smells sweetly of sawdust, freshly cut lumber and beeswax. The sun shines through a high window in the unused loft above, spilling a shaft of soft golden light across the coffin, turning the wood the color of honey. I run my fingers over the words burned into the plaque, fighting to keep my cool.

Our angel sleeps here.

For as long as the world spins and the earth is green with new wood, she will lie in this box and not in my arms.

"Goodbye, my angel."

ABOUT THE AUTHOR

Lurlene McDaniel began writing inspirational novels about teenagers facing life-altering situations when her son was diagnosed with juvenile diabetes. "I saw firsthand how chronic illness affects every aspect of a person's life," she has said. "I want kids to know that while people don't get to choose what life gives to them, they do get to choose how they respond."

Lurlene McDaniel's novels are hard-hitting and realistic, but also leave readers with inspiration and hope. Her books have received acclaim from readers, teachers, parents, and reviewers. Her novels *Don't Die, My Love*; *I'll Be Seeing You*; and *Till Death Do Us Part* have all been national bestsellers.

Lurlene McDaniel lives in Chattanooga, Tennessee.

You'll want to read

Letting Go of Lisa

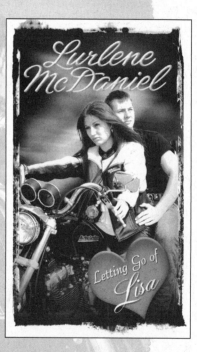

Lisa has a tragic secret, and when she decides
she'll handle it herself, Nathan has to
make a choice. Can he ever let go of Lisa?